Berries and Birthdays
Cove Cozy Mystery

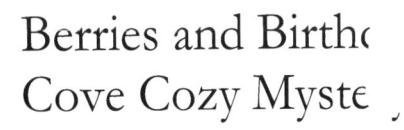

By Leena Clover

Copyright © Leena Clover, Author 2018

All rights reserved. No part of this publication may be reproduced, stored in a retrieval system, or transmitted, in any form, or by any means (electronic, mechanical, photocopying, recording or otherwise) without the prior written permission of the author.

This book is a work of fiction. Names, characters, places, organizations and incidents are either products of the author's imagination or used fictitiously. Any resemblance to actual events, places, organizations or persons, living or dead, is entirely coincidental.

CHAPTER 1	5
CHAPTER 2	17
CHAPTER 3	29
CHAPTER 4	42
CHAPTER 5	55
CHAPTER 6	68
CHAPTER 7	81
CHAPTER 8	94
CHAPTER 9	108
CHAPTER 10	121
CHAPTER 11	135
CHAPTER 12	148
CHAPTER 13	161
CHAPTER 14	173

CHAPTER 15	186
CHAPTER 16	200
CHAPTER 17	212
CHAPTER 18	226
CHAPTER 19	239
CHAPTER 20	252
CHAPTER 21	265
CHAPTER 22	278
EPILOGUE	288
OTHER BOOKS BY LEENA CLOVER	291
ACKNOWLEDGEMENTS	292
JOIN MY NEWSLETTER	293

Chapter 1

Jenny King fidgeted with her organza dress, trying to ignore the stream of sweat trickling down her back. Why had she ever agreed to be a bridesmaid, she moaned to herself. Could you technically be a bridesmaid if you were in your forties? The peach dress she was wearing was supposed to be pretty, but Jenny looked and felt like a giant pumpkin. The May morning was unseasonably hot, the temperatures already soaring above 95 degrees.

Jenny King was baking up a storm. A motley crew of people was helping her, each engrossed in their assigned tasks.

"What about the birthday cake?" Petunia Clark, the owner of the Boardwalk Café asked Jenny. "The Cohens are counting on you."

The small town of Pelican Cove was gearing up for a big July 4th celebration. It was a popular holiday in the seaside town, embraced by locals and tourists alike. A long list of events were planned and carried out with great enthusiasm every year.

This year was big for the town's oldest resident, Asher Cohen. It was his 100th birthday. Grand centennial celebrations were planned. Jenny was entrusted with baking the birthday cake.

Jenny King hummed a tune as she pulled out a pan of blueberry muffins from the oven. She reflected over the past few months of her life, realizing she hadn't been this happy in a long time. Jenny King had been a suburban mother for most of her life. One day, her husband of twenty years had come home and delivered a bombshell. He was going out with a much younger girl who was now in the family way. He asked Jenny to clear out.

Jenny had sought shelter on the remote island of Pelican Cove. Her aunt, Star, had welcomed her warmly and opened her house and heart to Jenny. After letting her mope and sulk for a few weeks, Star had cajoled Jenny into starting work at her friend Petunia's café. The rest, as they said, was history.

Jenny had started working her magic in the kitchen and now the whole town of Pelican Cove was singing her praises. People lined up to taste her food. Jenny didn't disappoint, coming up with delicious new recipes every few days, using the area's abundant local produce and fresh seafood.

"The cake's cooling over there," Jenny told Petunia, pointing toward a wire rack on the counter. "I already chopped the chocolate for the ganache."

"Aren't you making your special butter cream

frosting?" Heather Morse asked.

Heather was an islander who had become a close friend.

"Asher Cohen loves his chocolate," Petunia explained. Her double chins jiggled as she spoke. "He specifically requested a chocolate ganache for the cake."

"And Asher Cohen gets what he wants," Betty Sue Morse noted, her hands busy knitting a colorful scarf.

Betty Sue Morse was a formidable force in Pelican Cove. Her family had originally owned the island. It had been called Morse Isle then. She was the fourth generation descendant of James Morse who had travelled south from New England with his family in 1837. He had bought the island for $125 and named it Morse Isle. He built a house for his family on a large tract of land. Fishing provided him with a livelihood, so did floating wrecks. He sent for a friend or two from up north. They came and settled on the island with their families. They in turn invited their friends. Morse Isle soon became a thriving community.

Being a barrier island, it took a battering in the great storm of 1962. Half the island was submerged forever. Most of that land had belonged to the Morse family. A new town emerged in the aftermath of the storm and it was named Pelican Cove.

Heather was Betty Sue's granddaughter and the last of

the Morses.

"Give the man a break," Rebecca King or Star, Jenny's aunt, said. "He's turning 100, after all."

"And he can't stop reminding everyone about it," Betty Sue complained.

Asher Cohen owned a thriving construction business. He still maintained an active interest in every aspect of it. His money gave him power. He was one of the biggest employers in town and most people felt indebted to him because of it. Betty Sue Morse wasn't too happy about it. She felt the locals needed to worship the Morse name. Everyone else was an upstart.

"Don't be mean, Grandma," Heather said, scooping muffin batter into moulds. "Asher Cohen has been good for this town."

"He will never be one of us," Betty Sue Morse sniffed.

"Did he come from the Bella?" Jenny asked innocently. "I thought the Survivors were as good as locals."

Jenny was referring to the survivors of an old shipwreck. The summer of 1876 had brought tragedy to the island. A passing steamship, the Isabella, had sunk in the shoals. Plenty of people had gone down with her. There were only seventeen survivors who were rescued and brought to Morse Isle. They stayed on and never went back. Their families thrived on in Pelican Cove, still referred to as the Survivors. Star's deceased husband had been one of them.

"He appeared out of nowhere one fine day," Betty Sue told them. "Him and his wife and kid. Came around asking my Daddy for a job. I was knee-high to a grasshopper but I still remember."

"Grandma's right," Heather told Jenny. "He built Cohen Construction up from nothing. Now they are the best custom builders on the Eastern Shore. You couldn't have chosen a better company for your home."

Jenny had recently hired Asher Cohen's company to refurbish the ocean facing house she had bought with her divorce money.

"Mom!" a voice yelled from the deck out back.

"What is it, Nicky?" Jenny asked, peering out of the kitchen.

Her college going son Nick was spending the summer in Pelican Cove.

"How much watermelon do you think I can eat?"

"Plenty!" Jenny said, rolling her eyes.

Like most 19 year olds, her son had a voracious appetite.

"The twins say they can beat me at it."

Two lanky girls with eyes as blue as the ocean chortled with laughter.

"I can eat more than a girl," Nick grumbled.

He brightened as he spied a tall, muscular man walking up the steps from the boardwalk.

"What do you think, Adam?"

Jenny's heart raced as she feasted her eyes over Adam Hopkins. He was the sheriff of Pelican Cove and he did full justice to his uniform. Jenny and Adam had some turbulent history but they had called a truce and recently gone out on their first date. It had gone well.

Adam placed his arms around the two girls, his twin daughters. His eyes crinkled and little crow's feet appeared at the corners as he gave Jenny a mega watt smile.

"Why do you think I am so poor?" Adam asked Nick. "These two hellions have been eating me out of house and home all these years."

"But watermelon?" Nick asked. "Seriously?"

"Loser buys dinner," one of the twins said. "Deal?"

Adam and Jenny went inside, leaving the kids bickering about something else.

"How about a muffin?" Jenny asked. "They are fresh out of the oven."

"Can't say no to that," Adam said with a smile. "Have you finished baking for tomorrow? The races start in an hour."

"Why don't you go home and change, Jenny?" Petunia suggested. "We'll tidy up here and meet you on the beach."

"Do we have enough?" Jenny asked worriedly.

The Boardwalk Café was providing muffins and coffee for the entire town the next day.

"We do," Petunia assured her, dabbing the sweat on her brow with a handkerchief.

"Let the festivities begin," Star cackled, clapping her hands. "I can't wait."

"Grandma's flagging off the canoe race," Heather said. "We need to get going too."

"Tell me what the agenda is once again," Jenny sighed. "I don't know how you keep it straight, Heather."

"It's the same stuff year after year," Heather sighed. "That's why I'm excited about the centennial. It's going to be something new."

"Canoe races in the bay," Star counted off her fingers. "Fish fry at Ethan's after that. Bonfire on the beach. Breakfast at the Boardwalk Café tomorrow. Watermelon eating contest. Barbecue on the beach. Parade. Fireworks…"

"You missed the awards ceremony, Star," Betty Sue pointed out. "That's right after the parade."

"What about the birthday party?" Heather reminded them. "That's after the fireworks. We are all invited."

"You mean the centennial party," Jenny smiled. "Never thought I would be meeting a 100 year old man."

"He doesn't look that old," Star said critically. "And he definitely doesn't act that way."

"Careful, Star!" Betty Sue warned. "Are you angling to be his third wife?"

"Don't be silly, Betty Sue!" Star said, turning red.

They all shared a good laugh over that.

"I get off duty soon," Adam whispered to Jenny. "Can I pick you up after that? We can go see the races together."

"Jason's driving me there," Jenny said apologetically.

Adam's eyes flickered.

"Of course he is."

"It's not a date," Jenny said mildly. "He's just giving us a ride. I will see you there."

Jason Stone was a local lawyer, the only lawyer in Pelican Cove. He had gone out on a couple of dates with Jenny several years ago when she had visited the island as a teen. He still wanted to date Jenny King.

Light hearted and friendly, Jason had been a big help to Jenny when her aunt had been accused of a local murder. Jason was so easy going, Jenny loved spending time with him. He made her laugh, unlike the serious Adam Hopkins who made her blood pressure shoot up every time she exchanged a few words with him.

The whole town clapped and cheered the contestants of the canoe races. They gorged on all kinds of seafood at Ethan's Crab Shack after that where a massive fish fry was in progress.

Jenny hopped about with a smile on her face the next morning. They started the coffee around 8 AM, much later than usual. The doors opened at 9 to welcome the whole town.

"How long have you done breakfast for the town, Petunia?" Jenny asked.

"Every July 4th for the last 25 years," Petunia said proudly. "It's my way of doing something for them."

"People love the café, don't they?" Jenny beamed happily.

"More so now," Petunia nodded. "They can't stop drooling over your food."

Jenny tried to hide her blush as she flung their doors open.

Asher Cohen was the first person in line. He stood behind his wife, holding her wheelchair in his gnarled hands.

Jenny offered to wheel his wife in.

"Do I look senile?" he spat at her, then gave her a broad smile.

"Happy Birthday, Mr. Cohen," Jenny laughed, offering to shake his hand.

He held her hand in a tight grip and shook it heartily.

"How about some breakfast?" he asked, sitting at a table close to the door.

His wife didn't say much. Star had told her she avoided talking to strangers.

"Here you go, Mr. Cohen," Jenny said, bringing over a tray with warm muffins, butter, and two steaming cups of coffee.

"How's my birthday cake coming?" Asher Cohen asked. "Does it have the chocolate ganache like I told you?"

"Don't worry," Jenny assured him. "It's made exactly according to your instructions."

"I expect to see you at my party, young lady," he thundered.

Jenny tried not to stare at the shock of blond hair that covered Asher Cohen's head. His eyes were clear blue, only slightly clouded by age. He was pointing at her as he spoke, a habit he was well known for.

"Your party's the talk of the town," Jenny told him. "I'm not going to miss it."

"And make sure you watch the parade," he ordered. "I'm going to be riding in it."

A short, chubby man entered the café and sat next to Asher Cohen. His brown hair looked like it hadn't been combed that morning. His belly indicated how much he loved his beer. He scratched his head and tried to get the old man's attention.

"What's up, Gramps?" he grumbled. "I'm binge watching Game of Thrones. Why did you call me here?"

Asher Cohen grumbled something unintelligible.

"I need to talk to you, boy," he growled. "It's important."

Jenny noticed the woman in the wheelchair just by chance. Her fists were clenched so tightly they had turned red. The eyes staring at the chubby young man were full of an expression that could only be called hatred.

Chapter 2

The Main Street of Pelican Cove was decked out in red, white and blue. A recent beautification project had already made the town spiffy. Streamers and flags adorned storefronts, cars, trees, lamp posts, pillars and just about every available surface.

Jenny wore a flag tee with white Bermuda shorts and cheered wildly as the water melon eating contest started. Nick called it quits after his tenth slice of watermelon.

"What's next?" she asked Adam who was cheering for the twins.

"Are you hungry yet?" he asked.

"I'm starving," Jenny groaned. "I just had half a muffin this morning. We ran out! You won't believe the number of tourists that came through the café this morning."

"You can thank Instagram for that," Adam grinned.

"Or Mandy," Jenny said with a laugh.

The town of Pelican Cove had won the tag of Prettiest Town in America earlier that year, thanks to Mandy James, an enthusiastic consultant the town had hired.

She had started social media accounts for the town and literally put Pelican Cove on the map.

"Jason and Captain Charlie are manning the grill," Jenny said eagerly. "He's promised me one of his specials."

Adam Hopkins leaned on his cane and followed Jenny to a big tent that had been set up on the boardwalk. Jenny's friends, or the Magnolias as they called themselves, were seated at a big table in the center of the tent.

"We saved you a seat," her aunt called out. "You should try these hot dogs before they are gone, Jenny."

A tall, skinny woman with thick Coke-bottle glasses patted Jenny on the back as she sat down.

"Is that a new dress, Molly?" Jenny asked her.

Molly Henderson worked at the local library. She was closer in age to Heather Morse, at least ten years younger than Jenny's 44. But she had connected with Jenny instantly.

"I ordered it online," she said shyly. "How does it look?"

"It's perfect!" Jenny assured her.

"That's what I told her," a tall brown haired man

seated next to her exclaimed, making her blush.

"Why aren't you helping Jason at the grill?" Heather asked him.

Chris Williams stood up and stretched lazily. He ruffled Heather's hair and looked at her lovingly.

"I'm going, okay?"

"You better watch out, Heather," Jenny warned her. "Someone's going to snatch him from under your nose. Don't say I didn't warn you."

"Listen to her, girl," Betty Sue sighed. "Unless you want to be single at my centennial."

The women chattered on, jumping from one topic to another. Jenny tapped her foot impatiently, finding it hard to relax.

"Why don't you settle down, dear?" Petunia asked. "We've done our bit for the day. Time to sit back and enjoy."

"I'm going to get some food," Jenny said, getting up. "Coming, Molly?"

Jenny, Heather and Molly walked over to the grills and stood in line. There was a big variety of food to choose from, ranging from hot dogs, burgers and fish to an assortment of side dishes people had brought in.

They loaded big platters with a little bit of everything and carried them back to their table.

Heather placed a stack of empty plates next to the food.

Nick and the twins came by, feasting on giant candy floss on sticks. They promised Jenny they would eat some real food later.

"What is the parade like?" Jenny asked as she bit into a hot dog.

As promised, Jason Stone had mixed a special type of mustard to go with it.

"See for yourself," Star told her. "The big attraction this time is of course the Cohen Construction float. Asher Cohen is going to be on it."

"He told me about it this morning," Jenny nodded. "Say, who was the woman in the wheelchair?"

"That's his wife," Heather explained. "Linda Cohen."

"She's a Stone," Betty Sue called out.

Jenny wondered if she was related to Jason. She gossiped with Heather and Molly about the chubby man who had come to meet Asher Cohen.

"He's a ne'er-do-well," Heather said, "but he's the only

Cohen kid who's connected to the business."

"How many kids are there?" Jenny asked.

"You'll see some of them tonight," Heather shrugged. "Seven or eight…"

The girls went back to the grill for a second helping of everything, eating until they were stuffed to the gills.

Chris, Adam and Jason finally came over with their own loaded trays.

"That mustard was yum," Jenny told Jason. "You have to give me the recipe."

"When are we taking a kayak out?" he teased. "I'll swap the recipe for a date."

Jenny was deathly afraid of the water. As summer progressed, almost everyone had urged her to go fishing or bird watching with them. The thought of being so close to the water in a tiny kayak or canoe scared the bejesus out of her. She had been trying to hide her phobia from her new friends.

"It's peak tourist season," Jenny told Jason. "You know I can't get away from the café now."

"I can survive without you for a few hours," Petunia grunted.

"Maybe she just doesn't want to go out with you," Adam said seriously.

Jason knew about Jenny's date with Adam. Rather than discourage him, it made him more competitive.

"Jenny can choose for herself," he said curtly.

Adam struggled to his feet and excused himself.

"Look what you've done, Jason," Jenny protested. "Did you have to needle him?"

"Adam just needs an excuse to sulk," Jason shrugged.

"We need to go pick a good spot," Star spoke up. "Or we'll miss the parade."

She looked lovingly at Jason. She secretly wished Jenny would choose him rather than Adam.

"Are you done, boys? Let's go."

The group collected all their trash and disposed of it properly. They headed to Main Street, looking for a spot big enough for their whole group. Chris set up camp chairs for the older ladies. The others huddled around them as a band began playing.

"That's the high school band," Heather told Jenny.

The parade started soon after with the youngest

residents of Pelican Cove forming the vanguard. Kids in tricycles and bikes with training wheels pedaled onto Main Street. Red, white and blue streamers were tied to their wheels and handle bars. The crowd cheered wildly.

A contingent of senior citizens in motorized wheelchairs followed. The ponies were next.

"These are the famous Chincoteague ponies," Heather told Jenny. "They run wild on Assateague Island up north but some ponies are auctioned each year. The town owns a few of these. They are brought out during special ceremonies."

"I've heard about them," Jenny said eagerly. "But this is the first time I am actually seeing one of these."

"Haven't you been to Chincoteague yet?" Molly asked. "We should make a day of it, take a picnic basket with us. Girls only."

"Why girls only?" Chris teased. "What did we guys ever do to you?"

"Jenny and I went to Chincoteague for dinner a couple of times," Jason told them. "But going to see the ponies is a great idea."

"Pay attention, kids!" Betty Sue roared.

Fire trucks followed the ponies, festooned with

colorful ribbons. The marching band was next. The floats followed after that. There was one float for the City of Pelican Cove. It was covered in banners of the local businesses. The Boardwalk Café had donated one such banner.

"Look," Petunia pointed. "That's us!"

"Where's Asher Cohen?" Jenny asked. "Wasn't he supposed to be in this parade?"

"He's coming right up," Star said.

A red pickup truck brought up the rear. Large banners printed with Cohen Construction were attached to its sides. Bunches of balloons were tied to the rails every few inches. Asher Cohen stood in the back, waving at the people. A bunch of children stood around him, throwing candy in the crowd. Asher wore a festive red cap with the words 'Happy Birthday' festooned on it. The balloons had the word '100' written on them in glitter.

"They special ordered those balloons," Heather whispered. "Not many people celebrate their 100th birthday."

"You think?" Jenny asked sarcastically.

Asher Cohen blew a kiss to someone in the crowd. Jenny followed his gaze and saw the woman in the wheelchair smiling back at him. A young woman stood behind her, holding the chair.

Finally, the parade was over. Kids and grownups alike had scrambled to grab the candy. People stood around, chewing the sugary treats.

"I need to cool off," Betty Sue complained. "I could use some sweet tea right now, or lemonade."

"I made a pitcher of lemonade for us," Petunia told them. "Why don't we go into the café for a while."

She fanned herself with a handkerchief, looking as red as a tomato.

"I think we can all use a break," Jason agreed.

"I'm on duty for the next couple of hours," Adam spoke, getting up to leave.

Jenny breathed a sigh of relief as she let the air conditioning in the café cool her down.

"Has anyone seen Nick?"

"He got into a hot dog eating contest with some kids," Chris told them. "They were talking about taking some kayaks out after that."

Jenny shrugged. She reminded herself her son was an adult now and she didn't need to keep tabs on him.

"It's time for the awards ceremony," Betty Sue announced an hour later.

The older ladies had dozed off in their seats. Jenny and her friends had been indulging in some harmless gossip.

"Does everyone get an award?" Jenny asked, stifling a yawn.

"They try to cover most people," Star told her. "All the younger kids get something."

"Asher is bound to get Overall First Place today," Heather said. "They did a really good job with their float. All the lights were beautiful."

"He was just showing off," Betty Sue grunted.

Heather ignored her grandmother.

Betty Sue gave away some of the awards. There were squeals of joy as people showed off their trophies. Barb Norton, a local woman, held up a large brass plaque. The crowd roared in approval.

"And now, the Overall First Place Award for this year. Come on up, Asher. Come and get it."

People turned around, trying to spot Asher Cohen. There was a buzz at the back. The crowd parted to reveal the short, chubby man Jenny had seen with

Asher that morning.

"I can't find Grandpa."

The crowd started to speculate where Asher was. Some wondered if he had forgotten about the awards ceremony. Others made wisecracks about his age.

Adam Hopkins walked up to the makeshift stage and held up his hand. Jenny had a sudden feeling of déjà vu. She remembered a fateful party she had attended earlier that year.

"There has been an incident," Adam Hopkins announced. "I urge you all to calm down. My people will come around to ask you a few questions."

"What about the fireworks?" a voice called from the crowd. "The sun's going down. Can we head to the beach now?"

Adam went into a huddle with the people gathered on the stage. He turned around and cleared his throat before speaking again.

"The fireworks are cancelled."

The crowd protested loudly. One tourist pushed his way to the front and struck up an angry pose.

"What do you mean, mister? We travelled three hundred miles to spend our July 4th here. Our kids have been looking forward to the fireworks all weekend."

"I'm the Sheriff of Pelican Cove," Adam said in a clipped voice. "I am cancelling the fireworks for security reasons."

"What on earth is going on?" Jenny asked Heather.

The Magnolias had inched toward the podium. Heather scampered up the stage and conferred with Betty Sue. Her eyes were filled with alarm as she walked back toward Jenny.

"They just found Asher Cohen. He's dead."

Chapter 3

The Magnolias were on their mid-morning coffee break at the Boardwalk Café the next day. All the conversation revolved around Asher Cohen.

"Just imagine dying on your 100th birthday," Star was saying. "It's like someone jinxed him."

"Don't you mean hexed?" Molly asked.

"What a waste of that birthday cake," Heather sighed. "What happened to it, Jenny?"

Jenny shrugged.

"We delivered it to the Cohen residence the day of the party. I guess they will just throw it out now."

"Maybe we can bring it back," Heather said hopefully.

"Heather Morse!" Betty Sue exclaimed. "What are you doing hankering after a dead man's cake? Surely I raised you better than that?"

"I'll bake one for you, Heather, don't worry," Jenny consoled. "It's just a chocolate cake with a chocolate ganache and plenty of fresh berries on top."

"Stop! You're making me crave it even more."

"You girls are missing the point," Petunia said. "Why aren't we talking about what happened to Asher?"

"I'm not getting mixed up in a murder this time," Jenny announced resolutely.

Betty Sue sucked in a breath.

"Murder? Who said anything about a murder?"

"He was found dead in his car," Star reminded her.

"I thought he died from the heat," Betty Sue mumbled.

"The police aren't saying anything," Heather said. "They sealed off the crime scene pretty quickly. No one got a look at the truck."

"Was it the same truck that was in the parade?" Molly asked.

"I think so," Heather said.

She looked at Jenny with a gleam in her eye.

"When are you going out with Adam again? Maybe you can bend his ear about this."

"Have you met Adam?" Jenny asked with her hands on her hips. "He won't tell me squat."

"Don't change the subject, Jenny," Molly pounced.

"Are you going out on a date with Adam?"

"We were thinking of getting dinner tomorrow night," Jenny admitted.

"What about Jason?" Heather asked. "Have you dumped him now?"

"Jason and I are just friends," Jenny objected. "He knows that."

"Are you sure?" Molly raised her eyebrows. "I've seen the way he looks at you."

Betty Sue came to her rescue. Her knitting needles clacked as her hands twirled a strand of blue yarn over them.

"Stop harassing her, girls."

Nick ran up the café steps just then, waving an envelope in his hand.

"Mom!"

"What is it?" Jenny asked in alarm.

"It's that internship I was waitlisted for. One of the guys they hired dropped out."

"Is this that big law firm in Washington DC?" Jenny asked eagerly.

Jenny's ex-husband was a partner at a well known law firm. Nick wanted to follow in his footsteps. Jenny had developed an aversion to lawyers when her husband cheated on her. Then she met Jason Stone. She was beginning to think they were not all bad. Regardless of her personal beliefs, she fully supported her son in whatever he wanted to do in life.

Nick was looking excited.

"I won't be doing much, just getting coffee, I guess. But I'll be there, Mom!"

"When do you start?" Jenny asked.

"This coming Monday. But I need to look for a place to stay."

"Have you looked at online ads?" Molly asked.

"Not yet," Nick said, "but I'm going to."

"I've got my iPad right here if you want to look," Molly offered.

"Thanks Molly," Nick beamed, sitting down next to her. "This will save me time."

Jenny realized her son wouldn't be spending the summer with her after all. She rubbed the tiny gold heart shaped charm that hung around her neck on a chain and kept her thoughts to herself. Nick had started giving her a charm for Mother's Day since he turned eight. She had worn the charms on a bracelet for several years. Now she had strung them on a thin gold chain. They literally touched her heart, providing a tangible connection to Nick when he wasn't with her. She had fallen into the habit of rubbing those charms whenever she was worried or overwhelmed.

"We should have a family dinner before you leave," Jenny said. "I'm going to cancel my date with Adam."

"Why don't you invite him over?" Star asked. "It won't be a date but at least you will get to spend time with him."

"Sounds cool, Mom," Nick approved. "Can he bring the twins too?"

Jenny looked at her aunt speculatively.

"Do you want to invite Jimmy Parsons?"

Star looked at her incredulously.

"Why would I want to do that?"

"I told Jimmy to come around sometime but I doubt he's going to turn up on his own. This way, he'll have company."

Star gave a slight nod, making Jenny smile.

Jimmy Parsons was the town drunk. He lived in a tiny cottage by the light house on a deserted stretch of beach. The Parsons family had owned and operated the light house for years. The light house was decommissioned now but it was still a big point of interest in Pelican Cove.

Jenny had discovered Jimmy had a soft spot for her aunt. She was sure they shared some history. She was determined to find out more. Asking Jimmy over to dinner sounded like a great way to learn more about him.

Nick's voice snapped Jenny out of her reverie.

"What was that, Nicky?" she asked.

"Do you promise to stay out of trouble?"

"I'm supposed to ask you that!"

"You know what I'm talking about, Mom. You won't get mixed up in that old man's death, will you?"

"I barely knew the man, Nicky. Why would I get involved?"

The Magnolias looked disappointed. Nick didn't look convinced at all.

"Are you going to visit us on the weekends?" Star asked him.

Heather stood up and waited for Betty Sue to gather all her stuff.

"I need to feed Tootsie," she said, talking about her black poodle. "We have two couples checking in today."

Heather and her grandmother Betty Sue owned and operated the Bayview Inn. It was one of the oldest houses in town and had been built by James Morse himself.

The group broke up and Jenny went inside to get ready for the lunch rush. She started mixing her special chicken salad, made with fresh juicy strawberries. It had been a hit with the locals and tourists were lining up for it now.

Petunia helped her assemble the sandwiches. The talk turned to Asher Cohen again.

"Who found him, do you know?" Jenny asked Petunia.

"Why don't you go talk to Adam?" Petunia asked. "You can deliver lunch at the police station."

"Haven't we hired kids for that?" Jenny asked.

"The kids didn't turn up today," Petunia said. "Shouldn't matter to him."

Jenny placed a few sandwiches and cookies in a basket

and walked down the street to the Pelican Cove police station. One of the desk clerks, Nora, greeted her.

"Is that our lunch? I'm starving!"

Jenny stole a glance at the door marked Sheriff.

"He's in there," Nora said. "Alone. You can go right in."

Jenny rapped lightly on the door and went in. Adam Hopkins sat with one leg up on a chair. He was muttering to himself, trying to open a bottle of pills. Jenny took it from him and unscrewed the top.

"Your leg's bothering you today?" she asked softly.

Adam Hopkins had injured his leg in the line of duty. His recent stint of therapy had helped a lot, but the pain flared up sometimes.

"Had too much fun this week," he winced, popping a couple of pills in his mouth.

He washed them down with a glass of water.

"What are you doing here, Jenny?"

"I brought you lunch," Jenny simpered. "And I don't need a reason to come see you, Adam."

"You are sure this has nothing to do with Asher

Cohen?"

Jenny acted shocked.

"Don't expect any favors just because we are dating."

"Why would I? I know you well."

"And I know you, Jenny. That nose of yours is twitching as we speak."

"Who found him, anyway?" she asked. "Just out of curiosity."

"I did," Adam sighed.

"Was it heat exhaustion?" Jenny forged ahead. "The sun was scorching yesterday. It was ninety degrees in the shade."

"What do you care about Asher Cohen?" Adam asked, leaning forward. "Did you even exchange two words with him any time?"

"I knew Asher!" Jenny protested. "I baked his birthday cake. He put in a special order at the café. He tasted my food at Ada Newbury's party. His family hired a catering company from the mainland but Asher insisted I bake the birthday cake."

"That's all?"

"We met yesterday morning. He came to the café for breakfast."

Adam suddenly looked interested.

"How did he get there? Did anyone accompany him?"

"He came with that woman in the wheelchair. Heather said she's his wife."

"So he came in with Linda. Anyone else?"

"There was a chubby guy who came in some time later. He sat down with Asher."

"What were they talking about?"

"How would I know that?"

"Did you happen to overhear something?"

Jenny shook her head.

"I think the old man was berating him."

Adam had started to unwrap his sandwich as Jenny spoke. He took a big bite and gave her a thumbs up.

"Delicious, as usual!"

"Thanks," Jenny said. "So, did his heart give up? He seemed fine when he was standing up there on that float."

Adam refused to take the bait.

"About tomorrow," Jenny said. "We'll have to take a rain check."

"Is this how it's going to be?" Adam thundered. "You are punishing me because I won't answer your questions?"

Jenny threw back her head and laughed.

"Don't be silly, Adam. Nicky's got an internship. He's leaving the day after so we are having a family dinner. You are invited. So are the twins."

Adam looked relieved. He gave her a grudging smile.

"I hope you stay out of this Cohen business, Jenny. It might get awkward, what with you and me seeing each other socially."

"I have no intention of getting mixed up with the Cohens."

"Why are you asking all these questions then, hmm?"

"Just curious, I guess."

"You can read about it in tomorrow's paper."

"So you know how he died?"

"We are waiting on some reports, but I have a pretty

good idea."

"I can wait until tomorrow," Jenny said, standing up to leave.

She didn't want to push her luck.

Adam sighed as he took in her mulish expression.

"Okay, just this once."

"I'm not asking you anything," Jenny protested. "Let the record state that."

"This is not a courtroom, Jenny," Adam laughed.

He grew serious as he chose his next words.

"Asher Cohen died of carbon monoxide poisoning."

"Out in the open?" Jenny asked incredulously.

"We found him in the cab of his truck."

"Did you try to revive him?"

"He was already gone," Adam said grimly. "The paramedics tried their best."

"Did age have anything to do with it?" Jenny asked. "He was pushing a 100 after all."

"Asher Cohen was in excellent health," Adam told her.

"He might have lived for ten more years."

"What are you saying, Adam?" Jenny asked, aghast.

"Asher Cohen didn't die of natural causes," Adam said flatly. "Either he took his own life, or someone did it for him."

"But why?" Jenny cried. "He was such a sweet, old man."

She walked out of the police station in a daze. Asher had looked so happy, waving to the crowd, wearing that festive birthday hat. There was no way he would have taken his own life a few minutes later.

What was the alternative, Jenny asked herself. Had the town of Pelican Cove witnessed yet another gruesome murder?

Chapter 4

Jenny pulled a pan of blueberry muffins out of the oven. Captain Charlie, her first customer of the day was waiting in line.

"Good Morning," she greeted him. "What can I get you with your coffee?"

"Those muffins smell good," he said, breathing in the heady scent. "I've been eating muffins here all my life. But there's something special about these."

"I spice them up a bit," Jenny said, leaning forward to whisper in Captain Charlie's ear.

Jenny braced herself for the breakfast rush. Captain Charlie was always her first customer when they opened their doors at 6 AM. Her second customer of the day surprised her.

"Jason! What are you doing here so early?"

"I want to talk to you, Jenny," he said seriously. "It's important."

"Don't you have court today?"

"I've pushed a couple of my cases. I'm needed here."

Petunia had heard the exchange.

"Why don't you two go out on the deck? The tourists won't be here for at least an hour."

"Thanks, Petunia," Jason said with relief.

Jenny placed a couple of muffins on a plate and poured two cups of coffee. She led Jason out to the deck.

For once, Jason wasn't interested in the food. Jenny decided to take advantage of the respite. She cut a muffin in half and slathered it with soft butter.

"What's the matter? What's so important you couldn't wait?"

"Actually, I wanted to come over last night."

"Then why didn't you?"

"I heard about this family dinner you were having with Adam. I didn't want to intrude."

"You know you can talk to me any time, Jason. What's going on?"

"It's my aunt, Linda Cohen."

"Do you mean that lady in the wheelchair?"

"That's her alright. She had a stroke a couple of years

ago. Her right side is paralyzed below the waist. She can't walk."

"How are you related to her?"

"She's my father's cousin," Jason explained. "She was Linda Stone before she married Asher."

"Someone did mention that," Jenny nodded, taking a sip of her coffee.

Jason cut to the chase.

"She needs your help."

"Jason, I barely know her."

"Your reputation precedes you, Jenny."

Jenny popped the last piece of muffin in her mouth and quirked one eyebrow at Jason.

"I have a reputation? Nothing too bad, I hope."

"Are you being dense on purpose?" Jason railed. "I'm talking about your sleuthing abilities."

"And why does she need those?"

Jason swallowed some coffee and looked at Jenny.

"I don't know how much Adam told you. But it looks like Asher didn't die of natural causes."

"I know about that," Jenny admitted.

"Linda is concerned," Jason said. "You know how the local police operate. Being the spouse, she is bound to come under suspicion."

"Surely they won't suspect an invalid?"

"We don't know that," Jason sighed. "I'm going to provide her with as much legal aid as possible. But we have to be ready for any contingency."

"I think you have the bases covered," Jenny said. "Where do I come in?"

"Linda wants to find out what happened to Asher."

"I'm sure the police have opened an investigation."

"They have, but Linda wants you to look into this. She heard about the other cases you solved this year."

"I'm not a professional investigator, Jason," Jenny protested. "You know that. I was pulled into it by chance."

"She's my aunt, Jenny. Can't you please help us out?"

"I promised Nicky I wouldn't get involved," she told Jason. "He just left for the city."

Jason stood up and began pacing the floor.

"I suppose you promised Adam something too."

"Adam has nothing to do with this!"

"Just meet her once," Jason pleaded. "For my sake. That's all I am asking."

"Okay Jason, I will go meet Linda Cohen. No strings attached."

"Agreed," Jason said with relief. "When can you get away?"

"Not until later this afternoon," Jenny sighed. "I have a busy day ahead."

A large group of tourists came down the boardwalk and climbed up the steps of the café.

"I think that's my cue," Jenny said, getting up. "You can stay here as long as you want."

Jenny didn't get a chance to talk to Petunia until later that morning. The Magnolias arrived for their coffee break. Betty Sue was knitting something with green wool. Heather carried their black poodle Tootsie in her arms.

"She won't bother anyone," she promised Petunia. "I'll keep an eye on her."

"Is something wrong with her?" Jenny asked with

concern.

Her husband had retained custody of their aging terrier Cookie. Jenny missed him every day. She yearned for a pet of her own.

"Toots is a bit moody today," Heather explained. "So I brought her along."

Tootsie looked up when she heard her name and yawned.

Betty Sue and Heather pampered Tootsie and paid attention to her slightest yelp. She knew that very well.

"Jason was here bright and early," Petunia reported. "He was out here with Jenny for a long time."

"Hot date?" Molly teased.

"I wish!" Jenny smirked. "Linda Cohen wants to meet me."

"Didn't I tell you she was a Stone?" Betty Sue said, looking up from her knitting.

Star heard them discuss Jason's proposal as she walked up the café steps.

"You're doing it again, aren't you?" she asked.

"I just agreed to go meet her," Jenny explained.

Jason came to the café later to pick Jenny up. They drove up into the hills to a large estate.

"Isn't this where Ada Newbury lives?" Jenny asked, referring to one of the richest women in Pelican Cove.

"You're right. All the larger estates are in this part of town."

Jason drove through large iron gates and pulled up in front of an imposing three story colonial. A group of people sat in the living room. One of them waved at Jason and looked curiously at Jenny. Jason escorted her to a tiny elevator in an alcove.

"Asher had this put in for Linda," he explained.

The room Jason took her to had tall glass windows that provided a sweeping view of the ocean. Jenny spotted the lighthouse in the distance. Linda Cohen sat in her wheelchair, staring outside. She looked devastated.

"Hello Linda," Jason said, clearing his throat to get her attention. "We are here."

Introductions were made. Linda's face took on a hopeful look.

"Jason has told me a lot about you," she began. "He didn't have to, of course. Your food has made you famous. But people can't stop talking about how you solved those two murders."

"It was nothing, really," Jenny mumbled. "I just got lucky."

"Want to try that luck for me?" Linda asked.

Her eyes filled up and the expression on her face was so pathetic Jenny couldn't help but feel sorry for her. She took Linda's hand in hers.

"Mrs. Cohen, I am sorry for your loss. I only met your husband a couple of times but I liked him."

"He couldn't stop talking about that chocolate cake," Linda said with a smile. "He stole a slice as soon as you brought it over. Said it was his birthday. No one was going to tell him when to eat his own cake."

Jenny felt mollified.

"That's nice to know."

"Asher had an eye for people," Linda continued. "He said you were a smart cookie. You could dig yourself out of any hole."

Jenny looked at Jason pleadingly. He went and stood behind Linda and put his hands on her shoulders. She patted his hand, getting the message.

"I asked Jason to bring you here. I'll get to the point. I

need your help, Jenny. I want to know what happened to my Asher."

"The police…" Jenny began.

"I know the police are doing their thing. If I hadn't been stuck in this wheelchair, they would probably have carted me off by now. That's what happened to your aunt, isn't it?"

Jenny gave a slight nod.

"I'm not an investigator, Mrs. Cohen."

"Call me Linda, please."

"Okay, Linda. I just go around asking random questions. Some might think I browbeat them. There is no guarantee I will find anything."

"I know that," Linda said, leaning forward in her chair. "I am willing to take that risk."

"And I don't know what I will find," Jenny said next. "What if someone in your family comes under suspicion?"

"I don't care," Linda said strongly. "Whoever did this deserves to be caught."

"I can't stop working at the café," Jenny warned her. "Petunia depends on me. This is the busiest time for us."

"Jason explained all that," Linda said. "I won't be keeping tabs on you, Jenny."

"It's settled then?" Jason asked hopefully.

Jenny felt cornered. She didn't like to be put on the spot in this manner. At the same time, she was intrigued. One look around the room told her Asher Cohen had been loaded. Had someone killed him for money?

"I'll give it a shot," Jenny said weakly. "I just hope you don't expect miracles."

Linda grabbed Jenny's hand and thanked her profusely. Then she pleaded fatigue. Jason pressed a button and waited for a nurse to arrive. Jenny promised Linda she would come see her soon.

A tall, skinny man accosted them as they stepped out on the large wraparound porch.

"What brings you here, Jason?"

Jenny observed the man while Jason exchanged pleasantries with him. He was well preserved for his age. Jenny guessed it to be anything between 65 and 70. His head was sparsely sprinkled with blonde hair and his piercing blue eyes should have given her a clue to his identity.

"Jenny, this is Walt," Jason said, turning around to look at her.

"Walter Cohen," the man said, offering her his hand. "I'm the oldest son."

"Do you live here?" Jenny asked.

"Oh no. I am just here for the centennial. Or was. What a waste, huh? We traveled all the way from Florida and for what? Just to watch the old man croak?"

Jenny thought Walter's comment was in poor taste.

"Walter's your cousin?" she asked after they got into the car.

Jason drove out of the Cohen compound.

"Not exactly. Walter is Olga's son. That was Asher's first wife."

"What happened to her?"

"She died in childbirth, sometime in the 1960s."

"How did Linda come across Asher?"

"Linda has known him all her life. He went to work for her father when he first got here. My uncle taught him everything he knows about construction."

"He must have been old when he married Linda."

Jason agreed wholeheartedly.

"Some called it robbing the cradle. But Linda was in love with him. There was nothing to be done."

"How many kids did he have?"

"Five from the first wife."

"Five? And Linda took them on? How old was she at the time?"

"She's about Walter's age. The kids were grown. They didn't really need a mother."

"Does she have any kids of her own?"

"Three," Jason confirmed. "That's eight kids and who knows how many grand kids and great grand kids."

"That's a big family."

"Three generations over a span of a hundred years," Jason shrugged. "Sounds about right."

Jason himself had never been married. In his late forties, he had given up any hope of being a father.

"That's a whole lot of suspects," Jenny mused.

"You think someone from his family harmed him?"

"Greed is always a big motive, Jason."

"Want to get dinner somewhere?" he asked.

"It's been a long day. I think I just want to turn in early today."

"As you wish, Madame!" Jason said with a mock salute.

Star had cooked dinner. She dished up the steamed fish and chickpea salad Jenny liked.

"So you're putting yourself in danger again."

"She looked so distraught. I couldn't say no."

"What about your own life, Jenny?" Star asked, spearing a piece of fish with her fork. "You have the café, and the renovations at Seaview. When are you going to find the time to play Nancy Drew?"

Chapter 5

Jenny fried a batch of crab cakes for the Magnolias. It was crab season and most tourists ordered anything with crab in it. The Boardwalk Café was famous for its crab dip and crab salad sandwiches. Jenny wanted to up the ante and try something a bit more gourmet.

"They are here," Petunia said as she spied Betty Sue Morse walking in, clutching her knitting against her chest. Heather followed, biting her nails.

Jenny gently flipped the crab cakes in the pan and ladled them on a plate lined with paper.

"Have you tried this dipping sauce?" she asked Petunia.

Jenny had come up with a delicious mango chili sauce to go with her crab cakes.

"Our health conscious customers will love it," Petunia nodded happily.

"Let's see what the girls think about it," Jenny said, taking the platter of hot crab cakes out to the deck.

"Something smells yum," Molly said, breathing deeply.

"What's the matter with you, girl?" Betty Sue asked

Heather.

She had barely looked up when Jenny placed the plate of crab cakes before her.

Molly was smacking her lips as she licked the sauce off her spoon.

"You can bottle this sauce, Jenny," she crooned. "It's sweet, then it's hot, then it's sweet again. And that garlic!"

Molly's praise barely registered on Jenny's mind. She was looking at Heather.

"I'm going to start dating," Heather said suddenly.

"Does this mean you are going to take Chris seriously?" Jenny asked.

"It's about time!" Betty Sue snapped. "You have run that boy ragged."

"I'm not talking about Chris," Heather said in a small voice. "I want to see other people."

"Are you breaking up with Chris?" Molly asked incredulously.

"I've never gone out with anyone else," Heather burst out suddenly. "How do I know Chris is the right man for me?"

"He's held your hand in good times and bad ever since you were a kid," Betty Sue scowled. "That's how you know."

Heather looked at Jenny, begging her to understand.

"How do you want to go about this, Heather?" Jenny asked. "Join one of those dating sites?"

"I have no idea!" Heather cried. "I just need to go out with a guy who's not Chris."

"You're being a fool," Molly said flatly. "You'll never find anyone as good as Chris Williams."

"I want to find that out for myself," Heather said. "I want to go on a bad date."

"Do you also want to be mistreated by some idiot out there?" Molly asked, incensed. "Do you want to be rejected by someone who doesn't have a lick of sense?"

"Easy, Molly," Jenny said. "I kind of get what Heather's saying."

She sat down next to Heather and put an arm around her shoulders.

"What will you tell Chris?"

"I don't know," Heather sighed. "I haven't thought

that far."

"Then it's time you did," Betty Sue snapped, her needles moving in and out as she glared at Heather. "Think ten times before you hurt that poor boy."

Jenny changed the subject.

"What do you know about Asher Cohen?" Jenny asked Betty Sue. "You said something about him the other day."

"He came here after the big war with his wife and baby. Asked my Daddy for work. Wasn't skilled at anything. Old man Stone gave him a job. That's Jason's great uncle."

"He told me about that," Jenny nodded. "Were you friends with the Cohen kids growing up?"

"I didn't mingle much with those kids. Linda and I hung out for a while, although she was younger."

"She means she stuck to the Pioneer families," Heather clarified. "What a lonely childhood you had, Grandma."

"We did what we were told," Betty Sue grumbled. "We didn't go questioning our parents."

Jenny sensed another argument brewing.

"How are the crab cakes?" she asked her. "Have you tried one yet?"

"I thought I liked that strawberry cheesecake you made," Betty Sue said between bites, "but you have surpassed yourself, Jenny."

"Go ahead and write it up on the specials board," Petunia beamed.

"Maybe you should take some for Adam," Molly suggested, cutting into her third crab cake.

Jenny walked to the police station a couple of hours later.

"I brought you lunch," she told Adam, placing her straw basket on his table.

"Something smells good," he said approvingly.

"I met Linda Cohen yesterday," Jenny said, arranging three crab cakes on a bed of salad. She drizzled her special mango sauce over them and placed the plate before Adam with a flourish.

"Should I be worried?" Adam asked, cutting a crab cake into two.

"She looked so wretched, I couldn't say no."

"I see."

"You don't agree? I'm just humoring a poor widow. She can't do much herself, being indisposed."

"Who said I don't agree?"

"So you're cool with this?"

"I'm cool with anything, as long as you don't meddle in police work, Jenny." Adam wolfed down another big bite of the crab cake. "And you promise to stay out of trouble."

"It's not like I go asking for it."

Adam locked eyes with Jenny, giving her a scorching look. Jenny felt herself melt.

"You barely escaped some attempts on your life, Jenny. I couldn't handle it if something happened to you."

"I'm fine," Jenny said confidently. "All I'm going to do is ask some questions. Judging by the size of their family, I will still be asking questions in December."

Adam muttered something about the police doing better than that.

"These crab cakes are amaze, Jenny. I learnt that word from the twins."

"How are they doing? I miss Nicky already."

"Nick's rubbed off on them. Now they are looking for a job in the city too. I heard them talking about it last night."

"Any updates on Asher? Did you get the autopsy reports?"

Adam Hopkins was in a good mood. He didn't snap at Jenny.

"I sure did. And you won't be getting a look at them."

"Am I seeing you later tonight?"

"You might," Adam said, giving her a quick wink.

Jenny liked walking on the beach after dinner. The beach her aunt's cottage stood on offered one of the few flat stretches of shoreline in town. Adam went to the same beach with his dog Tank. Jenny and Adam had a standing date, unofficial of course, to meet on the beach every night.

Jenny walked out of the police station and decided to go meet Jason. She needed to get some background on Asher Cohen. Jason seemed to be the best source of information.

"Hi Jenny!" Jason greeted her. "Can I get you something to drink?"

Jenny opted for iced tea and Jason pulled out a bottle

from a small refrigerator.

"It's not fresh brewed like yours," he apologized.

"No problem," Jenny said, guzzling the cold drink.

"Are you busy right now?" she asked.

"I'm always busy," Jason sighed. "But it can wait. Tell me what's on your mind."

"What can you tell me about Asher Cohen? I thought you would know, since your aunt married the guy."

"I guess I know more than the townspeople."

"So tell me," Jenny said, leaning back in her chair and folding her hands.

"Asher Cohen came to Pelican Cove some time after the war. Late 1940s would be my guess."

"It was Morse Isle then, wasn't it?"

"You're right. The town of Pelican Cove hadn't been formed then."

"Did he come here alone?"

Jason shook his head.

"You remember his first wife, Olga? He came here with Olga and little Walter. Walt was just a baby, barely two years old."

"You weren't born then, were you?"

"Of course not," Jason rolled his eyes. "All of Olga's kids were born before me. I was just a few months old when Linda married Asher."

"You're rushing ahead," Jenny said. "Let's go back to 1948."

"Asher started looking for a job," Jason continued. "He had been an engineer before the war and he was a quick learner."

"Betty Sue said he went to her father for a job."

"I don't know about that," Jason said. "All I know is Linda's father, my dad's uncle, took him under his wing."

"He must have flourished," Jenny mused. "He had all those kids."

"Asher was smart. He gained some experience working with the Stone family. Then he set up shop for himself. Cohen Construction played a big part in the rebuilding effort after the big storm of 1962."

"Did your uncle resent him for it?"

"I don't know," Jason quipped. "I wasn't even born

then."

"What I mean is, did Linda's father face any losses because of this new business?"

"There was enough work for everyone," Jason said. "There was plenty of reconstruction up and down the coast. Cohen Construction handled it all."

"So the storm provided a windfall for Asher Cohen."

"Yes," Jason told Jenny. "He bought his estate around that time. He built that big house of his. But happy times didn't last."

"Is that when…?"

"Olga died in childbirth soon after. The youngest kid was ten at the time."

"That must have been a big blow."

"Apparently not," Jason shrugged. "Rumor has it Asher barely felt the loss. He married Linda a couple of years after that."

"How did that happen?"

"Linda was a child when Asher worked for her father. People say he was a handsome devil. Tall, blonde and blue eyed, he cut a fine figure. Success made him more attractive. When Asher swooped in to rebuild the town after the storm, Linda saw him as some kind of knight in shining armor. She had a big crush on him."

"Obviously, he must have returned her feelings."

"There was a big scandal," Jason laughed. "You know island politics. Linda was a Stone, a Pioneer. The families didn't like her hobnobbing with this foreigner."

"What about the kids?" Jenny asked. "Did they want a new mother?"

"I don't think Asher asked them what they wanted."

"Did they elope?"

Jason shook his head.

"That's one thing Asher seems to have been adamant about. He didn't want to leave Pelican Cove. He could have expanded his business a lot more if he set up shop in a bigger town. But he never left town."

"Did your family disown Linda?"

"They came around," Jason said. "Asher was her father's protégé after all. Linda's father trusted him. They tied the knot right here in town."

"How old was he at the time?"

"He was about fifty. Who knew he would live on to be a hundred?"

"And Linda has kids too?"

"Ryan, Scott and Dawn," Jason confirmed. "They were born in the 70s. Dawn's the youngest."

"Eight kids," Jenny exhaled. "That's some family."

"And none of them live in Pelican Cove."

"What about that chubby guy I have seen with Asher?"

"That must be Hans. He's Maria's son. She lives in New Jersey with her husband. Hans is the only grand kid to come and live here."

"Any reason why?"

Jason shrugged.

"You'll have to ask them."

"Would you say Asher was a family man?"

"I think so," Jason said. "He always complained about how none of the kids had time to come visit."

"Sounds like he led an ordinary life," Jenny observed. "Lots of widowers remarry, so I don't see anything special there."

"What are you looking for, exactly?"

"A motive, Jason. Something that might indicate why someone would want to kill Asher Cohen."

"Still waters run deep, Jenny. Who knows what lies beneath the surface?"

"You're right," Jenny said. "I need to talk to the Cohen clan, at least those that are present here."

Jason offered to go with her.

"Let's do that tomorrow. Do we need an appointment?"

"I don't think so, but I'll ask Linda."

"I don't want to raise her hopes, Jason."

"Any action is progress," Jason told her. "Who knows what you might find?"

"Do you really think one of the Cohen kids had a motive?"

Chapter 6

Jenny sat on the edge of her seat, trying to think of what to say. Walt Cohen lounged in an armchair before her.

"I hope you don't mind a few questions," she said timidly.

Walter looked relaxed in his khaki shorts and Hawaiian shirt. He rubbed his hand over his balding head and looked at Jenny.

"I don't. Can't say the same about the others."

"Can you tell me something about your father?" Jenny began. "Were you close?"

"I am the oldest of eight," Walt said. "I think he expected me to take over the business. But I took up a government job as soon as I finished college."

"You don't like the construction business?" Jenny asked.

"I got tired of living in this town," Walt said frankly. "You just got here, right? You have lived your life elsewhere. You can't imagine growing up in a small community where everyone points fingers at you."

"Why would they do that?"

"My Dad had nothing when he got here. Then he grew richer than some of the oldest inhabitants of this island. That was reason enough, I guess."

"Anything else?"

"I was always the foreigner's kid. I never really made any friends here."

"You're saying the locals are xenophobic?"

"Aren't they?" Walt quirked an eyebrow. "Anyhow, the government was recruiting when I graduated from college. I got a nice 9 to 5 job in the city and I took it."

"Are you retired?"

"That's another thing I didn't agree with the old man about," Walt said. "I stopped working as soon as I could. I had no intention of working until I took my last breath."

"You mean Asher hadn't retired yet?"

"Officially, he had. But he liked to keep a foot in the door."

"Where do you live? Do you visit Pelican Cove often?"

"I live in Florida in a posh retirement community. My

wife and I are happy there. Our kids live all over the country. They come visit us for holidays. We hardly get a chance to come here. The centennial was an exception. We were planning this for the last couple of years."

"Are you close to your siblings?"

"My sister Emma lives near us. We meet often. The others, not so much."

"What about Linda's kids?"

"My kids are closer to them in age. They keep in touch online."

"Did your father have any enemies?"

Walt let out a sigh.

"My father spent his life in an isolated town. He immersed himself in his work. He had no friends to speak of, other than Linda and her family."

"Could he have rubbed anyone the wrong way?"

"As far as I know, my father minded his own business. He wasn't a big talker. He would go fishing in his spare time."

"How is the business doing? Surely you have a stake in it?"

"I never cared for the business. I saved enough to retire comfortably. I don't care what happens to the business."

"You do know someone harmed your father?"

"It must have been a mistake," Walt said, shaking his head. "The old man led such a boring life, I can't imagine anyone having a beef with him."

"Did he ever visit you in Florida?"

Walt grew thoughtful.

"That was another of his quirks. He never left Pelican Cove. It was as if the transatlantic journey finished him. He hated travel."

"Did he visit his homeland again?"

"He didn't like to talk about it," Walt told Jenny. "That was one subject which was always taboo."

"Your Mom didn't want to go either?"

"My Mom was with him on that one," Walt said curtly. "They never wanted to go back."

"Bad memories?"

"Something of that sort," Walt shrugged.

"I would like to talk to your siblings," Jenny said. "Are

they around?"

"Most of us are," Walt told her. "Emma and Heidi were in the sun room earlier. I don't know about the rest. Ask the maid."

The maid came by just then and stood next to Jenny. Walt went out.

The maid escorted Jenny to the third floor. Linda was in a wheelchair, staring out at the sea.

"How are you, Jenny?" she smiled.

"Have you learned anything more, Linda?"

"The police haven't said much. I think they are stumped."

Jenny marveled at Linda's chiseled face. She had good bone structure. She didn't look much older than sixty but Jenny figured she was much older.

"I talked to Walt."

"Walt and I played together as kids," Linda said. "Asher used to bring him over when he came to visit my Daddy."

"Did you always want to marry him?"

"Not at first," Linda reasoned. "I guess I had a crush

on him at 15. But he was a married man."

"Did Walter resent you for taking his mother's place?"

"You'll have to ask him that," Linda shrugged. "The older three were almost my age. Maria and Paul took to me. They were young enough to be impressionable."

"Could any of the kids have held a grudge against Asher?"

"For marrying me?" Linda burst out. "Surely they would have said something about it?"

"Walt said none of the kids live here."

"Who can blame them?" Linda squared her shoulders. "There's nothing much to do here. You know that! They didn't see a future here so they found jobs and went away."

"Aren't they interested in the family business?"

Linda narrowed her eyes.

"I think Maria is. That's No. 4. She's sent her son Hans to live with us."

"Is that the chubby man who was with you at the café?"

"That's him alright," Linda said tersely.

"You don't like him?"

"He's not exactly the brightest bulb in the box. He's lazy and he drinks a lot."

"I think I get the picture. Why did Asher hire him then?"

"He's family!" Linda said simply. "Asher really wanted some of his kids to join him in the business."

"What about your own kids?"

Linda brightened at the mention of her children.

"Ryan's the oldest. He's about Jason's age. He's a colonel in the army."

"Was he here for the party?"

"Oh no! He's stationed overseas. He couldn't get away."

"Who else?"

"Scott's next. He's a doctor in a big hospital. He lives in New York City."

"Do they have kids?"

Linda shook her head.

"Ryan's wife left him. Couldn't adjust to the lifestyle. Scott is a widower. He never remarried. Dawn's little girl is my only grandchild."

"Dawn is your youngest?"

Linda nodded.

"She lives on a homestead in rural Maryland. I think the town she lives in is smaller than Pelican Cove."

"Is she here?" Jenny asked.

"Dawn is here with her husband and her little girl," Linda smiled. "They went for a picnic on the beach."

"Can I talk to Walt's siblings?"

"They should be around somewhere."

Linda was looking pale all of a sudden.

"Do you have a nurse to look after you?"

"Asher always took care of me himself," Linda told her.

Her eyes filled up and she looked away. Jenny said bye and beat a hasty retreat. She walked around on the first floor, trying to locate the sun room.

She heard some women talking and followed the sound. Jenny walked into a hexagonal room with tall stained glass windows. Three women sat in wicker chairs, presiding over a pot of tea.

"Hello dear," one of them spoke up. "Are you looking for someone?"

The woman who spoke was a female version of Walt. She was dressed in a similar fashion too. Jenny noted her white shorts and Hawaiian style shirt.

"Are you Walt's sister?" she asked.

"Emma Cohen," the woman nodded.

She pointed at a plump, white haired woman seated next to her.

"This is Walt's wife."

The attractive blonde seated next to Emma spoke up.

"I'm Heidi, Walt's other sister. How can we help you?"

"My name is Jenny. I live in Pelican Cove. Actually, I just moved here a few months ago."

Jenny realized she was babbling and tried to curb herself.

"Let the girl settle down," Emma said, giving Heidi a stern look.

"Linda wants me to look into what happened to

Asher."

"He was a hundred years old," Heidi dismissed. "He died."

"You do know how he died?" Jenny asked.

She wondered if Heidi was being obtuse on purpose.

"I guess he wanted a last hurrah," Heidi smirked. "He was always an attention seeker, our Dad."

"You think he took his own life?" Jenny asked. "That's not what the police think."

"Do you work for the police?" Emma asked. "Or are you a private eye?"

"Neither," Jenny admitted. "I'm just doing this for Linda."

"And what exactly are you doing?" Heidi demanded. "Are you going to browbeat us into admitting something nasty?"

"Of course not!" Jenny said, aghast. "I think we got off on the wrong foot."

"What do you want from us?" Emma asked.

"I'm talking to everyone in the family," Jenny explained. "I want to understand Asher as a person."

"He was an arrogant prick who lived alone and died alone," Heidi snarled. "That's all you need to know."

"Do you agree with her?" Jenny asked Emma.

Emma was quiet.

"Walt said you live near him in Florida?"

Emma perked up.

"We live in the best retirement community. It's so pretty. We have a big pool and we are just two miles from the beach."

"Did you think of living in Pelican Cove?"

"Walt and I have always been close," Emma said. "We bonded after our mother died. I took care of the younger kids, you know, being the older girl in the family."

"What about you?" Jenny asked Heidi. "Never wanted to live in Pelican Cove?"

"I got out of this shit hole as soon as I could," Heidi said with relish. "I wanted to see the world. I was a stewardess for an international airline."

"You weren't too crazy about your Dad, huh?" Jenny asked bluntly.

"I stopped talking to him the day he married Linda."

"Surely you were just a child then?"

"I was 14. Plenty old enough to understand he didn't have to replace our mother."

"Don't be silly, Heidi," Emma sputtered. "That was a long time ago."

"I never forgave him," Heidi grunted.

"So I guess you didn't visit much?" Jenny asked.

"My husband was a pilot. We live in Arizona now. Our kids work on the West coast so there's hardly any reason to come here. We see Walt and Emma when we go to Florida."

"We all agreed to come here for the centennial," Emma added. "We have been planning this for a long time. Daddy was really excited about seeing us."

"He must have missed his children," Jenny mused.

"I think Daddy was really unlucky in that aspect," Emma agreed. "He had eight kids and over a dozen grandkids. But he hardly ever saw them."

"Don't forget Hans," Heidi spit out.

"Other than Hans," Emma agreed. "But he's Hans."

So far, Jenny hadn't heard a single good thing about the chubby man.

"Did your father have any enemies?"

"He wasn't that important," Heidi scoffed. "He was just a sorry old man living in some obscure small town in the middle of nowhere. Who had the time to think about him?"

Jenny realized Heidi had plenty of unresolved issues about her father. She wondered if she had said the same things to the police when they questioned her.

"Can you think of someone who had a grudge against your father?" she asked Emma.

Emma looked thoughtful.

"Let me call for a fresh pot of tea," she said, pressing a bell. "My mind works better with a cup of tea."

Chapter 7

Jenny sipped her chilled white wine and sampled the crab cake. She was having dinner with Jason at a fancy seafood restaurant in Virginia Beach. They had been there before and it was fast becoming their favorite.

"You give them a run for their money," Jason commented as Jenny chewed a tiny piece of the crab cake.

"We get the freshest crabs," Jenny observed. "Probably better than what these people get."

"So?" Jason asked, taking a sip of his drink. "Shall we make it official?"

Jenny fought a blush but acted innocent.

"What do you mean, Jason?"

"Is this our first date, Jenny King?"

Jenny's response was to take a big gulp of her wine.

"Your divorce is final, Nick's doing fine, you just bought the house of your dreams, the café is doing well … can you squeeze a little bit of time to start dating?"

"We've been out to dinner like ten times, Jason," Jenny argued.

"But you said those weren't dates," Jason pointed out. "When do we officially start dating?"

"Do we need labels?" Jenny asked, trying to divert Jason. "Why can't we go on as we are?"

"There's a line I won't cross, can't cross, unless we are on an official date."

"Jason Stone, you're just a big flirt!"

Jason laughed wholeheartedly. Jenny had to admit he looked very attractive.

"You can stall all you want, Jenny, but I'm going to wear you down one of these days."

Dinner proceeded at a leisurely pace. Jason held the door for her and played her favorite music in the car. They pulled over at the scenic outlook on the Chesapeake Bay Bridge-Tunnel.

A pale yellow full moon rose over the water. Jenny enjoyed the view, letting the gentle waves of the Bay calm her. The inky water shimmered in the moonlight, and Jenny inched closer to Jason, putting her head on his shoulder.

"I've never stopped here at night," she admitted. "It's a

beautiful sight."

"You know what they say?" Jason whispered. "Virginia is for Lovers."

Jenny had a spring in her step the next morning. She added a double dose of cinnamon to her muffins and made a streusel topping.

"You're looking chipper," Captain Charlie grunted as he picked up his coffee and muffin.

"It's a wonderful day, isn't it?" Jenny gushed. "I watched the best sunrise on my way to work."

Jenny was in the habit of seeing the sun come up over the ocean every morning on her way to work. On a clear day, one could see the big orange ball of the sun splashing the sky in shades of red, pink and mauve.

"How was your meeting with the Cohens?" Betty Sue asked her later over coffee.

Star was sketching something on a piece of paper, barely paying attention. Her head jerked up when she heard the Cohens mentioned. Her hair was windswept as usual and Jenny wondered where she had spent her morning.

"Are you set up by the marshes again?" she asked her aunt.

Star shook her head.

"I'm out by the lighthouse. I'm out of all my lighthouse pictures. They are flying off the shelves this year."

Star had a small gallery where she sold sketches and paintings of the surrounding area. Summer was a busy season for her, with tourists flocking to buy paintings of the ocean and the marshes.

"Are you putting your new paintings online like I showed you?" Jenny asked.

Star nodded. "I sold a few pieces online this week. I can't keep up with the demand."

"Demand is good," Molly said. "You can start a waitlist and offer some kind of incentive."

"Forget about that for a minute," Star dismissed. "What's this about the Cohens?"

"We didn't get a chance to talk," Jenny explained to her aunt. "I met Linda again. And I met some of the Cohen kids."

"Kids!" Heather sniggered.

"Stop it, Heather," Betty Sue ordered. She leaned forward with interest. "Did you meet Walt?"

"Walt seemed a bit aloof," Jenny reported. "Heidi was angry. I think she's been mad at Asher her whole life."

"You're missing the point," Molly interrupted. "Ask her about her date with Jason."

"We don't have to," Heather said, pointing at Jenny. "She's turning red."

Jenny walked to the seafood market after work. Chris Williams was stacking shelves. His face broke into a smile when he spotted Jenny.

"Hey Jenny! How are you?"

Jenny chatted with Chris for a while.

"When do I get to taste your crab cakes? Heather can't stop singing your praises."

His face clouded over when he spoke about Heather. Jenny wondered if Heather had told him about her crazy dating idea.

"All well?" she asked.

"Has Heather talked to you about us?"

Jenny hesitated.

"She wants to date other people," Chris burst out.

"I think she's confused," Jenny said.

"I'm not," Chris said strongly. "I was getting ready to propose. This thing has thrown me out of whack."

"I'm sure Heather loves you, Chris."

"She has a fine way of showing it," Chris smirked. "Why is she acting out?"

"You know what I think? I think you should let her have her way."

"I've always imagined growing old with Heather. What if she finds someone else?"

"She won't," Jenny assured Chris. "But if you don't let her do this, she'll always wonder."

"What if she goes out with a scumbag?" Chris asked. "I won't be there to look out for her."

"She can take care of herself. Maybe she needs to prove that to herself."

Chris packed a pound of shelled and deveined shrimp for Jenny.

"So I should just wait for her to come back to me?"

Jenny picked up some fresh sea bass and handed it to Chris.

"That sounds best."

Jenny had a surprise in store for her when she got home. Jimmy Parsons sat on the porch with her aunt. He was dressed in shorts and a faded shirt. His clothes were old but they looked freshly washed. That was quite an improvement. Jimmy himself looked like he had showered and shaved.

"I asked Jimmy over for dinner," Star said hesitantly. "Do we have enough?"

Jenny held up her shopping bag.

"There's plenty to go around, don't worry. Why don't you two catch up? I'll take care of dinner."

Jenny chopped garlic and made a marinade of freshly squeezed orange juice, paprika and fresh dill. The sea bass went into it for five minutes before getting seared in a hot pan. Jenny doused the shrimp in Old Bay seasoning and added a squeeze of lemon juice and oil. She added it to another hot pan.

Star had cooked some brown rice. Jenny made a quick rice salad with blueberries and dill. She sliced the yellow tomatoes Betty Sue had grown in the inn's garden.

"What's new with you, Jimmy?" Jenny asked as she served dinner.

Jimmy Parson's reputation as the town drunk preceded him. But Jenny had no idea what he did for a living.

"It's tourist season," he said, biting into a plump shrimp. "Lots of chores to keep me busy."

Jenny debated asking about the chores. Star came to her aid.

"Jimmy rents out some cottages to the tourists."

"Oh?" Jenny exclaimed. "I didn't know that."

"The Parsons family lost a lot of land in the big storm," Jimmy said, sipping his sweet tea. "We only have half a dozen cottages now, scattered across the island."

Jenny understood who funded his drinking habit.

"I didn't know you had family on the island."

"My nephew's wife and kids live here," he nodded. "He's away most of the time, working on a rig. My baby sister lives in Atlanta with her husband. We hardly ever see her."

Jenny was shocked to learn Jimmy Parsons wasn't the hobo she had thought him to be. She had to learn to look beyond appearances.

Star must have read her thoughts because she gave Jenny a withering look.

"Star tells me you're looking into Asher's death?"

Jimmy asked. "He was a good man."

"You knew Asher Cohen?" Jenny asked.

The day was full of surprises.

"We were buddies," Jimmy said softly. "We went fishing in that creek on his land. We sat around for hours, shooting the breeze."

"Any idea who did this to him?"

"Asher didn't take crap from anyone. But he was a fair man. He provided a lot of employment for people up and down the coast."

"What about his kids? Do you know them?"

"I knew Paul growing up. That's the youngest of Olga's kids. He left town as soon as he finished high school."

"What about Hans? Maria's son? Did he hang out with you and Asher?"

"That kid?" Jimmy snorted. "He's married to the bottle. Hangs out at the Rusty Anchor most of the time. Drinks on the job too."

"I bet Asher didn't like that."

Jimmy forked a big piece of fish into his mouth and

shook his head vigorously.

"Asher couldn't stop stewing over it. Called him out for it too."

"Shouldn't he have fired him?"

"Blood's thicker than water, I guess," Jimmy shrugged. "And Maria would have given him an earful. She's the only one of Olga's kids who comes to visit."

"What about Linda?" Jenny asked. "Do you know her?"

"Jimmy and Linda are the same age," Star supplied. "Jimmy dated her in high school."

Jimmy Parsons turned red.

"Ah! It was just puppy love, Star."

He gave her a meaningful look. A silent message passed between the older couple. Jenny tried to hide a smile.

Star had baked a berry pie for dessert. They sat on the porch, eating big slices of the warm pie topped with vanilla ice cream.

A large yellow Labrador came bounding up the beach. He jumped up on the porch and put his paws on Jenny.

"Tank, you monster! Let me eat."

Tank butted her with his head and barked happily. A whistle sounded in the distance. Adam Hopkins walked up slowly, barely leaning on his cane.

"Hello everyone. Tank, stop bothering Jenny."

The yellow lab plopped down by Jenny's feet and put his head on her knee. She put her plate aside and fondled him.

"Care for some pie?" Star asked.

"I shouldn't," Adam said, staring at her plate.

"Why don't you sit down?" Star laughed. "I'll bring you a small piece."

Jimmy seemed uncomfortable in Adam's presence. He gobbled up his dessert and said goodnight.

"Did I drive him away?" Adam asked.

"Maybe."

"How's your little project going, Jenny?"

Jenny didn't take the bait.

"Very well. What about your investigation?"

"You know I can't talk about that, even if I wanted

to."

"Have you found a motive yet?"

Star came out with a plate of pie in her hand.

"What happened to Jimmy? Did you scare him away, Adam?"

Adam shrugged.

"I didn't say a word."

"You have that effect on people," Jenny teased. "Most people are intimidated by you."

"But you're not one of them," Adam said with a hint of a smile. He took Jenny's hand and wove his fingers through hers. "I'm glad."

Star cleared her throat.

"Did Jenny tell you about her date with Jason?"

"It wasn't a date," Jenny protested. "Just dinner."

"You keep telling yourself that, girl!" Star sighed and went inside.

"How about a walk?" Adam asked.

Jenny nodded. Tank scampered after them. They set off the motion detectors at Seaview. The three storey house Jenny had bought recently lit up like a Christmas tree. The scent of roses and gardenias perfumed the air as Jenny leaned against the gate to admire her new home.

"When do you finish repairs on Seaview?" Adam asked.

"The work's stalled," Jenny told him. "They barely started."

"Oh yes, Cohen Construction is doing your renovations, right?" Adam asked. "I forgot about that."

"Asher went over the plans himself," Jenny said sadly. "He was excited. He said he would give it his personal attention since I was involved."

"Who's going to oversee the work now?"

"I don't know," Jenny said. "I forgot to ask."

Chapter 8

"How about meeting at the Rusty Anchor later tonight?" Heather asked Jenny. "We need to talk."

"Have you…" Molly asked, looking interested.

"Later!" Heather cautioned. "We'll talk later."

The Magnolias commented on some of the tourists and devoured the lemon blueberry muffins Jenny had baked that day.

"It's getting too hot," Star complained, pulling off her paint splattered smock. "I feel like adding ice to my coffee."

Jenny liked the idea.

"You read my mind. I was thinking of offering iced coffee on the menu. Some people asked for it."

"That's it then," Betty Sue stated, placing her knitting down on the table. "We are drinking iced coffee until summer winds down."

"Can you make mine a frappe?" Molly asked.

"Well, I'm no barista," Jenny said modestly, "but I can try."

The girls met at the local pub that evening. Heather ordered the first round of drinks.

"I did it," she beamed. "I downloaded one of those dating apps. I created a profile too. Now I just need to upload a picture."

"Use an old picture," Molly said. "That's what everyone does."

"You mean, like, one from my college days?"

Molly nodded vigorously. "You want to look young. Younger than you are, that is."

"I don't think that's a wise move," Jenny said disapprovingly.

The girls argued over the photo, finally calling a truce. Jenny snapped a picture of Heather and they uploaded it.

"What happens now?" she asked Heather.

"Now we wait, I guess."

"You don't have to," Molly said. "You can express interest in other guys."

"How do you know so much about this?" Jenny asked, her hands on her hips. "I'm beginning to think you have done this before."

"Not exactly," Molly said evasively.

A chubby man with a protruding beer belly was seated at the bar.

"Isn't that Asher's grandson?" Heather asked. "Hans something."

"Maybe you should date him," Molly kidded. "I heard he's single."

"Hush," Jenny said. "I need to talk to him."

She walked over to the bar and held her hand out.

"I'm Jenny King. You are Asher's grandson, aren't you?"

"So what?" he asked belligerently.

He took a deep sip of his beer and belched. Jenny tried to keep a straight face.

"Linda's asked me to look into Asher's death. So I am talking to people."

"What's that?" he asked, peering at her through red eyes.

Jenny decided he had already knocked back a few drinks.

"I talked to your aunts and uncles. I would like to ask

you some questions about Asher."

"You some kind of detective?"

"Oh no! I run a café in town."

The man's frown turned into a smile.

"That's right. You're that cake lady. Grandpa couldn't stop talking about his birthday cake."

Jenny smiled and nodded.

"What do you want to know?" Hans said, draining his beer.

He called for another.

"Can we go get a table?"

Hans grabbed the mug of beer and led her to an empty table at the far end of the room.

"Err…I didn't get your name," Jenny began.

"Hans Geller."

"How long have you lived here in Pelican Cove?"

"I spent a lot of summers here, growing up," he told her. "Mom always came here to visit Gramps. I started working at the business a couple of years ago."

"You like the construction business?"

"It's not bad," Hans shrugged, hiccupping loudly.

"Can you tell me something about your grandpa?"

"He was old!" Hans sniggered and started coughing.

"Other than that," Jenny said with a smile.

"He was a skilled carpenter," Hans said. "He made music boxes. You know the ones? Music plays when you open the box. It was cool."

"Did he teach you how to make them?"

"He tried," Hans said. "But I'm not into that kind of thing."

"What about Linda?" Jenny asked.

"She's my grandma."

"She's not related to your mother though?"

"Linda's always been my grandma," Hans said, looking uncertain.

"You know what happened to Asher, don't you?" Jenny asked delicately.

"He died, dude!" Hans said.

His speech was becoming slurry but he continued to drink.

"I mean, you know how he died?"

Hans looked back at her blankly.

"Did he have any enemies?"

"Why would he? He was such a sweet old man."

"Can you think of someone who might have wanted to harm him? Someone who might have argued with him recently?"

Hans looked jubilant as he connected the dots.

"Luke, of course. Luke and Gramps didn't get along at all. Luke was trying to steal the business from him."

"Who's Luke?"

"He likes to think he's the head honcho over at Cohen Construction. But he's just a hired hand."

"Why did this Luke fight with your grandpa?"

"It was about me," Hans said proudly. "Luke went behind my back and told Gramps I drank on the job."

"Did you?"

Hans gave her a sheepish grin.

"I might have, once or twice."

"What did your grandpa do?"

"I'm still here, aren't I? Grandpa gave him an earful."

"You think this Luke hated your grandpa?"

"You're not very sharp, are you? Luke hates *me*! He's on my case all the time."

Jenny ignored the barb at her.

"We are talking about who might have hated your grandpa."

"Why would anyone hate him?" Hans asked. "He had money. Tons of it."

"What do you do at the construction business?" Jenny asked, trying a different tack. "Are you a foreman or something?"

"I came here to be a foreman," Hans said with anguish. "You think I came to this hell hole of a small town to unload trucks?"

Jenny sensed a tirade coming.

"Gramps made me foreman on a job but that Luke went and told him I almost cut myself with a saw."

"That sounds dangerous."

"Luke said I couldn't use any power tools until I cleaned up."

"Looks like he's looking out for your safety."

Hans snorted and rolled his eyes.

"He's looking out for himself. He wants to steal the business."

"How can someone steal a business?"

"Luke's been at it for years. He acts like he owns everything."

"What about Asher's kids?"

"My aunts and uncles? They couldn't care less. They didn't exactly get along with Gramps. Aunt Heidi hated him."

"So your Mom was the only one who came here to visit?"

"She's smart," Hans said. "She said she did it for me. She hates Pelican Cove."

"So you don't like working at Cohen Construction?"

Hans drained his beer and tried to lift his arm to call for another.

"You've had enough for tonight, buddy," Eddie

Cotton called out from the bar.

Hans muttered a string of profanities, making Jenny cringe.

"I'm getting out of here," he roared. "Saying goodbye to this crappy town."

"Where will you go?"

"Back home, of course."

"Where were you on July 4th? I didn't see you up on the float with Asher."

"That float looked amaze, didn't it? I decorated it, with the little kids. Gramps said I did a good job."

He seemed genuinely happy about the compliment.

"Why didn't you ride the float with everyone else?"

"I was out buying more booze for the party. Gramps was worried we didn't have enough. The whole town was coming, you know."

Jenny's aunt had helped plan the party. She had an idea how grand it was. The town had provided the food and Asher had insisted on footing the bill for the drinks.

"Asher was having a good time," Jenny remembered.

"He looked so happy in that birthday hat."

"I got him that hat," Hans boasted. "Gramps showed me a picture. I went to the city to get one in red, just like he wanted."

His chubby face finally showed some emotion. His eyes filled up and his mouth puckered, making Jenny wonder if he was going to cry.

She turned around at the sound of her name.

Heather and Molly were trying to get Jenny's attention. She thanked Hans for his time. Hans put his arms on the table and burrowed his head in them. Jenny heard a faint snore as she walked away.

"What took you so long?" Molly asked.

"That was Asher's grandson."

"Jenny," Heather said, grabbing her arm to get her attention. "Look here. I pressed the Like button on a few of these profiles. A couple of them Liked me back. What do I do now?"

Jenny laughed, shaking her head.

"Don't ask me! I'm too old for this stuff."

"Of course you don't need this stuff," Molly griped. "You have two handsome hunks falling all over you."

"Come on…not that again!"

"Heather has a guy too, of course," Molly continued. "I'll never understand why she's doing this."

"I met Chris," Jenny told Heather. "He seemed sad."

Heather was busy browsing through photos of eligible men. The girls split up after some time and Jenny walked back home. She was going to collect a pizza for dinner.

Jason Stone was at Mama Rosa's, waiting for his order.

"Hey, beautiful!" he whispered, giving her a hug. "How's the sleuthing going?"

"Not that great," Jenny told him. "I just met Hans at the Rusty Anchor. He's leaving town."

"You mean leaving for good?"

Jenny nodded.

"That's not what I heard," Jason said in disbelief. "Hans has his eye on the business. He wants to take over."

"He said someone called Luke was giving him a hard time."

"Luke's doing that?"

"Who is he anyway?"

"Come on Jenny. You know Luke. He drew up the plans for your remodel."

A tall, hefty man with black hair swam before Jenny's eyes.

"You mean that guy who was with Asher? The one with that large mole on his cheek?"

"That's Luke alright. It's a birthmark, not a mole."

"How do you know him?"

"Luke's my uncle. I thought you knew that, Jenny."

"Is he related to Linda then?"

"Of course! He's her brother. Luke Stone."

"How long has he worked for Asher?"

"Since he was a kid. He's the main force behind Cohen Construction."

Jenny reflected over her conversation with Hans Geller.

"Hans is not too crazy about that, I guess."

"Luke called him out on his drinking. Asher wasn't too pleased with Hans. Luke and Hans don't see eye to eye."

"Could you say he has a grudge against Luke?"

Jason nodded.

"Most people who work at the company know that. Hans is on cloud nine now. He thinks he's going to inherit."

"Is he?"

"The will hasn't been read yet. I can't comment on it at this time."

"But you know what's in it?"

Jason looked uncomfortable.

"It's my job to know, Jenny. I have been handling Asher's affairs since I came back to town."

"Don't worry. I won't ask you to do anything unethical."

Jason's order came up.

"I have to go. I have an early meeting on the mainland."

Jenny picked up her pizza and worked out different scenarios in her mind on her way home. If Luke had been the victim, Hans would have made a great suspect. She wondered why Hans had lied to her about leaving town.

She hoped the will would be read soon. That would give her an idea about who benefited most from Asher's death. She still hadn't come across a tangible motive for killing a 100 year old man.

"You're home!" Star cried from the front porch. "I'm starving."

They decided to eat their pizza on the porch, enjoying the view. Jenny bit into the cheesy slice, rubbing the tiny gold heart that hung around her neck. She missed her son. He had sent her a couple of text messages since he left but they hadn't talked. Her phone rang just then and a beloved face flashed on the screen.

"Nick!" she cried, putting him on speaker phone. "I was just thinking about you."

"How are you, Mom? Are you missing me yet?"

"You scamp!" Star roared. "You better get your butt out here this weekend."

Chapter 9

Jenny warmed chocolate and cream in a double boiler. She stirred the chocolate until it became glossy and poured it over a chocolate cake that was cooling on a wire rack.

"Is that for me?"

Heather had just come in followed by Betty Sue. Her eyes bulged and she looked like a child who had been offered a surprise treat.

"I was craving cake too," Jenny said, tossing some berries in powdered sugar.

She began placing them on the cake.

"Summer Fest is coming up," Betty Sue said, twirling a strand of blue wool around her needles. "We need to lock down some things."

"Why don't we talk about it today?" Petunia asked, picking up a jug of coffee.

The outside of the jug was wet with condensation. Ice cubes tinkled inside.

"Is that the iced coffee you were talking about?" Betty Sue asked Jenny. "I'm ready for some."

Star and Molly came in just then and the Magnolias went out to the deck.

"What's the special attraction for Summer Fest this year?" Star asked.

Petunia and Betty Sue were co-chairing the festival committee. They had plenty of volunteers but they were responsible for making the big decisions.

"We will have a bouncy house," Betty Sue said. "A lot of the parents asked for it last year."

"How about a Ferris wheel?" Star asked. "It's been ten years since we had one."

Jenny was preoccupied with thoughts of Asher Cohen.

Heather waved a hand before her eyes.

"Hello! Did you hear what I just said?"

Jenny shook her head. She looked at Betty Sue.

"Where did Asher Cohen come from? No one's ever talked about that."

"Switzerland," Betty Sue spoke up. "I had never heard of it. Daddy showed it to me on the globe he had in his study."

"So he was Swiss?"

"Don't be daft," Star said. "He was German, or must have been."

"I am going to talk to Linda," Jenny said decisively.

"Why don't we go get some of that cake?" Heather said, giving Jenny a meaningful look.

Heather whipped out her phone as soon as they entered the kitchen.

"A guy wants to meet me. Look!"

She pulled up a picture of a tall, good looking guy. Jenny thought he looked a lot like Chris Williams.

"He lives in Maryland. He's coming to Ocean City with his friends for the weekend. He says he can drive down here to meet me."

"You'll meet him once," Jenny said. "What about after that? Are you going to travel all the way to Maryland to see him?"

"I haven't thought that far," Heather said sullenly. "What's the harm in meeting him in Pelican Cove?"

"Doesn't sound too risky," Jenny admitted. "You can bring him here or take him to the Rusty Anchor."

"Shall I say yes?" Heather beamed. "It's a date!"

She sent off a quick message. Jenny saw a smiley face pop up on Heather's screen.

"Don't tell Grandma about it."

"How old are you, Heather? 16?"

"I don't want her nagging me about it. She goes on and on about how great Chris is for me."

"She's not wrong."

"Maybe not," Heather said crossly. "But if I hear one more word about Chris, I'll just lose it. I'm going to meet Duster and have a good time."

"Duster?" Jenny stifled a laugh. "I'm sure you will."

Jenny drove to the Cohen home by herself. Jason hadn't returned from the mainland yet. The maid asked her to wait in the living room.

Emma Cohen walked by, wearing a filmy cover up over a swimsuit. Jenny hoped her body would have that kind of tone when she was seventy.

"Oh, it's you," Emma said. "Here to see Linda?"

Jenny nodded. "Do you have a beach on your property?"

"At the far end," Emma told her. "But it's strewn with

rocks. We have an Olympic sized swimming pool. Dad swam twenty laps every morning."

"He looked quite fit for his age," Jenny observed.

"There was nothing wrong with him," Emma said strongly. "We may have had our differences, but my father was a good man. I hope you help us find out what happened."

"I'm not a professional," Jenny told her, "but I am going to do my best."

She hesitated.

"The other day…I didn't think you were keen on my asking questions about Asher."

"I was playing it cool for Heidi. She likes to say she hated Dad but that's not true. She does hate Linda though."

The maid came in to escort Jenny up to the third floor.

"We are all grieving," Emma said suddenly. "We just have different ways of showing it."

Linda was seated in her usual spot by the window. Jenny thought she had aged in the last few days.

"You are okay here, aren't you?" Jenny asked her. "I mean, you feel safe here?"

"Why wouldn't I?" Linda asked, surprised. "This is my home."

Jenny debated what to say.

"Did Walt say something to you?" Linda asked. "The older kids never accepted me. I think they weren't young enough to think of me as a mother. Even a stepmother."

"It doesn't bother you?"

"It used to," Linda admitted. "But I learned to live with it. All the grandkids call me Grandma though. We agreed on that."

The maid came in with a tray of drinks.

"You like lemonade, don't you?" Linda asked. "I took the liberty of ordering some for us. It's such a hot day."

Jenny thanked her and took a deep sip.

"I was thinking about Asher's past," she began. "Can you tell me something about his past life?"

"You mean his life with Olga?"

"Not exactly," Jenny said. "I mean his life before he came to Pelican Cove."

"Asher was very secretive about it," Linda said slowly. "Whatever little I know, I pieced together over the years."

"Betty Sue said he came here from Switzerland?"

"That's true. Walter was born there. He's the only one of Asher's kids who wasn't born in the States."

"What did he do in Switzerland?"

"He worked in some mill, I think. It was a hard time for them. Asher and Olga starved themselves and saved every penny they could. It took them four years to earn enough to buy a passage to America."

"Was he Swiss then? My aunt said he was German."

Linda gave Jenny a long look.

"I think he went to Switzerland from Germany. I don't know if he was German though. He could have been brought there from just about anywhere. Poland, Hungary, who knows."

"What do you mean, brought?" Jenny asked.

"He didn't like to talk about it," Linda said. "He never told me anything about his family or his childhood. All I could gather was that he must have come from money. He spoke English really well so he was educated. He had really great manners. And he was smart. I think he was an engineer. That's why my Daddy took him on as an apprentice."

"Did he have any siblings?"

Linda shrugged.

"He may have. But they are all gone. He barely escaped himself."

Jenny felt her head buzz with sudden clarity.

"Wait a minute, Linda. Was Asher a Holocaust survivor? Is that what you are saying?"

"I thought you knew," Linda said. "Although he never admitted it in so many words. He just never talked about that part of his life."

"It must have been painful."

"That's what I thought too. I didn't press him about it."

"Isn't it amazing? He built a whole new life for himself and lived to be a hundred!"

"I still can't believe Asher is gone," Linda said, wiping her eyes. "He was so full of life. He was looking forward to the centennial. He planned little details. He wanted everything to be perfect."

"Have you remembered anything?" Jenny asked her. "Someone with a grudge, any arguments he may have had?"

Linda shook her head.

"Can you tell me about Luke?" Jenny asked, putting her glass down on a side table. "Jason said he's your brother."

"Asher raised him as his own," Linda said. "Luke is a lot younger than me. We lost our parents in an accident a few months after I got married. Luke came to live with us."

"When did he join the business?"

"He used to tag along with Asher when he was in school. He never worked any place else. Asher depended on him."

"I talked to Hans," Jenny admitted. "He didn't seem too pleased with Luke."

"Hans is a spoilt brat. Maria dumped him here when she got tired of getting him out of scrapes. He drinks and gambles and picks fights. Asher worried about him."

"Did Luke ban him from the construction sites?"

"Hans had a narrow escape. He almost cut himself

fatally. Luke said he was a hazard to himself and the people around him."

"I don't think Hans is too happy about that."

Linda shrugged.

"Asher was with Luke on that one. Luke's been running the business for years. Asher semi-retired at 82."

"So Luke and Asher got along well?"

Jenny observed Linda's face when she asked that question.

"Of course," Linda said quickly. "In some ways, Luke was closer to Asher than my own kids."

"Do you know who's going to inherit the business?"

Linda smiled.

"I have a general idea, but I may be wrong."

"Why?" Jenny asked, suddenly alert. "Did Asher change his will recently?"

"He was planning to make some minor changes."

"I need to know who benefits from the will."

"Most of our kids are doing well," Linda said. "The

older ones are comfortably retired. I don't think Asher's will is going to make a difference."

Jenny chatted with Linda for a while and took her leave.

"Why don't you come over to the café sometime?" she hinted. "You can sit out on the deck and watch people on the beach. There's a lot of tourists around now."

"Asher used to take me around," Linda said sadly. "Luke and Jason have both offered. Maybe I'll come visit one of these days."

Jenny ran into Heidi on her way out. Heidi was wearing a robe over a two piece swimsuit. Jenny admired her skirtini.

"Any progress?" she asked Jenny.

"Some," Jenny said. "I'm trying to learn more about Asher's past."

"Dad never talked about it," Heidi said. "He didn't want the horrors of his life to cast a shadow on us. We learned about the war in school. That's when Walt told us where Dad had been."

"He must have wanted to spare you the pain."

Heidi shrugged and stalked away.

Jenny stopped at the police station on her way home. Adam was dealing with some paper work.

"What brings you here, Jenny?" he asked.

"Have you made any progress in the Asher case?" she asked.

"We can talk about anything but that," Adam said patiently. "I'm about to finish up here. Why don't we go out to dinner? I heard of a nice place in Cape Charles. We can watch the sunset over the Chesapeake."

"Please, can you throw me a bone? I'm stumped."

"We are waiting for the will to be read," Adam conceded.

"You want to follow the money trail," Jenny nodded. "I thought of that too. When are they going to do it?"

"I think they are waiting for some of the kids to turn up. The one who's overseas can't make it. But there's a doctor in New York and another guy somewhere in the Midwest. They should both be arriving any time."

"What about Linda's daughter?"

"She's here," Adam confirmed. "You haven't met her yet?"

"I met the swimsuit sisters," Jenny said with a laugh. "Wait till you run into them."

Adam gave Jenny a smoldering look.

"We should go swimming some time. We can take a canoe out to one of the barrier islands."

Jenny quailed at the thought of being on the water.

"Yeah," she agreed. "We should do that."

Chapter 10

Jenny rubbed the soles of her feet, trying to fight a wave of exhaustion. She had made dinner plans with Jason but she was feeling drained. It had been a busy day at the café. The tourists loved the new iced coffees and frappes on the menu. They had sold thrice the amount of coffee they normally did.

"Why don't you stay in?" Star asked, chopping cucumber for a salad. "I'm sure Jason won't mind."

Jenny scrunched her face and shook her head.

"I need a change of scene."

Jason arrived just then. He was dressed casually. Jenny surmised he must have had time to go home and change.

"You look tired, Jenny."

Jenny waved off his concern.

"I need some fresh air. I've been cooped up at the café far too long."

"I know just the place," Jason quipped. "Shall we?"

Jenny was surprised when Jason pulled to a stop

outside Ethan's Crab Shack. Ethan Hopkins was Adam's brother.

"Hey Jenny, Jason!" Ethan greeted them.

Jenny couldn't help smiling back.

Ethan was Adam's twin but they couldn't have been more different. Ethan boasted a paunch and his blue eyes twinkled merrily without effort. He didn't seem to carry the weight of the world on his shoulders like Adam.

"You wanted fresh air," Jason said. "And I figured you weren't up to a long drive. So I brought you here."

"You're the best, Jason," Jenny said, planting a kiss on his cheek.

"You want the House Special?" Ethan asked and they both nodded enthusiastically.

Jenny suddenly felt very hungry. She grabbed a table near the water while Jason collected their beers. Ethan brought over a platter of fried mozzarella sticks, hush puppies and onion rings.

"Fish is coming right up," he promised.

Jenny gorged on the hush puppies and the cheese sticks, dipping them in Ethan's special marinara sauce.

"So tell me what's new, Jenny. How goes the search?"

"I spoke to Linda again," she told Jason. "I had no idea Asher came here from Germany."

"He didn't talk about it," Jason said. "You know how the local hierarchy works. I guess being a foreigner in Pelican Cove was hard enough."

"Luke's name keeps coming up. I think I should go and talk to him."

Jason was looking toward his right. He smiled and waved at someone.

"You are in luck," he said, turning toward Jenny. "Luke's right here."

"Is he alone?" Jenny asked, turning around. "I don't want to interrupt his dinner."

"Let me go talk to him," Jason said, getting up.

He came back five minutes later.

"It's all set. We can talk over dessert. Luke doesn't mind."

Ethan brought over their beer battered fish and shrimp just then. Jenny spotted something peculiar on the platter.

"Soft shell crabs," Ethan announced. "These are my first batch of the season. You're going to love these, Jenny."

Jenny devoted herself to doing full justice to the tasty meal. She vowed to walk extra to work off all the grease.

"You're perfect just the way you are," Jason said softly.

"How do you always read my mind?" Jenny groaned.

"I have special powers," Jason grinned.

"Let's call Luke over."

A tall, hefty, brown eyed man ambled over to their table. He slapped Jason on the back and sat down next to him.

Jenny introduced herself to him.

"Linda's told me about you," he told her.

"You don't look like Jason's uncle," Jenny blurted out.

Luke Stone had the same angular face and chiseled features as Jason. But he didn't seem much older. Jenny tried not to stare at the black spot on his left cheek.

"I'm about thirteen years older than him," Luke told

her. "Stone men age well. It's in the genes." He jerked his thumb toward Jason. "Hold on to him, young lady."

Jenny tried to hide a blush. She rushed ahead with the first thing that came to her mind.

"So you are the head honcho at Cohen Construction?"

"You've been talking to Hans, haven't you?" Luke winked. "Only he uses those words."

"I didn't mean any disrespect," Jenny mumbled.

"That's fine," Luke reassured her. "Asher handed over the reins to me many years ago. In fact, my time there is almost up."

"What do you mean?"

"I'm looking forward to retirement," Luke explained. "Five more years at the most. Then it's me and my fishing rod."

"What will happen to the business?"

Luke shrugged.

"Frankly, I couldn't care less. Asher was good to me, and so was the business. I'm grateful for that. But I won't be wielding a saw forever."

Ethan brought over big bowls piled high with peach cobbler. There was a generous scoop of vanilla ice cream on top.

"This is a family recipe," he told Jenny proudly. "Our grandmother learned it from her grandmother. I may not be a fancy baker like you but cobbler is one thing we do right."

He waited until Jenny tasted the warm, sweet dessert. She moaned with pleasure and gave him a thumbs up.

Ethan went back to the kitchen with a broad smile lighting up his face.

"Did you ban Hans from the business?" Jenny asked Luke.

"I wish," he sighed. "Asher would never allow that. Nor would I let it happen, for that matter. I bounced that young man on my knee, you know. I hate to see him make a mess of his life."

Jenny waited for him to go on.

"There was an incident with a power saw. Hans almost lost his hand."

"Was he drunk on the job?"

Luke nodded.

"He's drunk pretty much all the time. I think he might have a drug habit too. I banned him from using any power tools. It was a safety measure."

"Did Asher know about this?"

"He ordered it," Luke said. "He was losing his patience with Hans."

"But Hans thinks you want him out of there."

"I don't mind being the bad guy," Luke shrugged. "We all tried to talk to him. Asher, Linda, his mother. He won't listen."

"Any reason for his discontent?"

"He wanted to control the business. Asher said no way."

"Did they fight over it?"

Luke seemed hesitant to reply.

"Hans has neither the knowledge nor the experience to head a business like Cohen Construction. Hundreds of people depend on it for their livelihood. He will run it into the ground in no time."

"So Asher depended on you. Did you get along well?"

"Well enough," Luke said casually. "But I hated the

man. I never forgave him."

Jenny gave a quick glance at Jason. He didn't look surprised by Luke's statement.

"Err...what are you talking about, Luke?"

"He ruined my sister's life," Luke spat. "She spent her whole life in Pelican Cove, looking after his kids. Never even crossed the state line."

"Does Linda feel the same?" Jenny asked, aghast.

"She doesn't realize what she lost!"

Jenny took a big bite of her cobbler and tried to process what Luke was saying.

"So you didn't like Asher Cohen, huh?"

"Like? I couldn't stand the sight of him."

Jason muttered something under his breath and looked away.

"I thought you were friends," Jenny said meekly.

"He was my mentor," Luke nodded. "He took me in when I lost my parents. I know I owed him a lot. But I still hated him."

"You mean you hated being beholden to him?" Jason suggested.

"No. I worked hard my whole life, gave everything I had to the business. I think I paid him back many times over."

"You just hated him," Jenny repeated. "Where were you on the day of the parade? I don't remember seeing you in the crowd."

"I was picking up some lumber for an urgent job," Luke said. "Actually, Hans was supposed to do it but he didn't turn up. Asher told me to go instead."

"Can you think of anyone who might have hated Asher?" Jenny asked. "Other than you, that is."

"He got along with most people," Luke said grudgingly.

"Did he fight or argue with anyone recently? Did anything out of the ordinary happen at work?"

Luke shook his head.

"Asher was a generous employer. He paid above the market rate and took care of his people."

"What about his other kids?" Jenny asked. "Do you suspect any of them?"

"Linda's boys are too busy," he said, counting off his fingers. "Walt and Heidi talk big but that's just their way of getting attention. Dawn is so exhausted most of the time she's just happy to put her feet up when she comes here."

"What about Emma?"

"Emma's always been the peacemaker. She keeps Walt and Heidi in check."

"Anyone else?"

"Have you met Todd yet?" Luke asked. "He's a smooth operator. Always after another handout."

"Who's Todd?" Jenny asked, making a mental note of the name.

"He's Dawn's husband," Luke said. "He'll do anything for money."

Luke stood up before Jenny could say anything more.

"Look, I appreciate your doing this for Linda. One thing's for sure. Asher's gone and Linda is finally free."

He turned around and walked out.

Jenny looked at Jason.

"That was intense!"

"Luke doesn't mince words."

"What was all that about hating Asher?" Jenny asked.

"Does he realize what he's saying?"

"You think Asher's killer would go around declaring his feelings? Luke's harmless."

"I wonder what the police think about him."

"Go ask Adam," Jason joked. "You are thinking of him, aren't you?"

"What? Of course not, Jason."

"Prove it," Jason said. "Let's go for a moonlight canoe ride."

Jenny shivered with apprehension.

"Anything but that," she croaked, shaking her head.

"Is that something you're planning with him?" Jason asked.

"What's the matter with you, Jason?" Jenny asked tearfully.

She stood up and picked up her bag.

"Please take me home," she said curtly.

Jason paled as he looked at Jenny.

"I was just kidding," he said. "Really. You think I feel threatened by Adam Hopkins?"

Jenny barely spoke to Ethan as she walked out.

"Jenny?" he called after her. "Is everything alright?"

Jason hurried after her and got into his car. They drove back in silence. Jason stopped in front of Star's cottage ten minutes later.

"Jenny, I'm sorry," he pleaded. "I don't know what I said to hurt you, but I'm sorry."

"I'm tired, Jason," Jenny sighed. "We'll talk tomorrow."

Jason watched her rush inside. He was puzzled by her behavior.

"What have you done, boy?" Star asked from the porch.

Jason hadn't noticed her.

"She's mad at me," he said with wonder. "I said something about Adam and she flew off the handle."

"Lord have mercy…" Star mumbled under her breath. "I wouldn't worry about it," she consoled Jason. "She'll be fine tomorrow."

"Are you sure?"

"Yes, I'm sure," Star snapped. "Now go on home and

get some sleep."

Jenny came out after Jason left. She had changed into some sleep shorts and a tank top. She sat down next to Star. Star stroked her back and waited for her to speak up.

"Is he mad at me?"

"Jason's a good man," Star said. "He was worried about you."

"Jason asked if I was thinking about Adam. I don't know what came over me."

"Were you?" Star asked her, holding her chin up. "Were you dreaming about that Hopkins boy while having dinner with Jason?"

"Ethan was right there!" Jenny argued. "How can I not think of Adam when his photo copy is hovering around me?"

"They may be twins but they are nothing alike. You know that, sweetie."

"I guess it was wrong."

"I don't know," Star said. "But losing your temper was."

Jenny felt she understood why Heather wanted to date

other people. She herself had married her college sweetheart. She had never really dated anyone. Now she had two men vying for her attention but she had no idea how to behave with either of them.

"I need a Duster," she said suddenly, making Star raise her eyebrows in question. "I have no idea what to do on a date."

Chapter 11

Heather Morse was about to burst. She tugged at Jenny's arm and almost pulled her into the café's kitchen.

"I did it," she screeched. "I met Duster yesterday."

Molly had followed them in.

"So you went on that date after all."

Heather looked like the cat that swallowed the canary. She didn't need any encouragement.

"We met at a small diner up the coast. I didn't want anyone in town telling on me, you see."

"How was he?" Jenny asked, unable to hide a smile.

Heather hadn't looked this upbeat in a long time.

"He was nice," Heather beamed. "His family is renting a house on the beach somewhere off the Chesapeake Bay. He invited me to spend a day with them."

"Are you going?" Molly asked. "You shouldn't go alone."

"Will you go with me?" Heather asked eagerly. "Duster has a bunch of cousins. They do this every summer, it seems. Rent a big house somewhere and get together."

"Will I need to take a day off?" Molly asked uncertainly.

"Not unless you want to," Heather said. "We can go up there this Saturday."

She started tapping the keys on her phone.

"It's all set. They are expecting us."

"Have you told Chris about this?" Molly asked.

"I told him yesterday," Heather nodded. "He's cool. We are meeting for drinks at the Rusty Anchor later tonight."

"You make my head reel," Jenny said as she walked back to the deck.

"How's that young man of yours, Jenny?" Betty Sue asked, busy knitting a pink scarf.

"Which one?" Star asked and the old ladies sniggered merrily.

Jenny spotted a familiar figure walking on the beach.

"Isn't that Hans?" she said aloud. "What's he doing here at this time?"

She wondered if Luke Stone had fired the young man.

"Why don't you take this over to the police station?" Petunia asked later, handing her a heavy basket. "We have ten lunch orders from them today."

Jenny was secretly thrilled at the thought of seeing Adam. She had missed her after-dinner walk for a couple of days and hadn't run into Adam.

"Care to have lunch with me?" Adam asked her as she placed her basket on his table.

The entire staff at the police station was busy gorging on her sandwiches and cake.

"There isn't enough food for the both of us."

"Are you sure?" Adam asked with a twinkle in his eye. "Why don't you look in that basket again?"

"There's an extra sandwich here!" Jenny exclaimed. "And two slices of cake. But how could this be? Petunia packed the lunches herself."

A gleam came into her eye as she spotted Adam's smug expression.

"Adam Hopkins! Did you plan this?"

"Can't blame a man for trying," he said, shrugging his shoulders. "It's hard to snatch you away from your friends."

"I've just been busy," Jenny apologized. "You know it's peak tourist season. And then there's Linda."

"Yes, Linda," Adam mumbled, rolling his eyes. "How's that coming along?"

"As a matter of fact," Jenny began, "I did have a few questions for you."

Adam held up a hand.

"No shop talk until we finish eating. After that, I will listen to whatever you have to say about the Cohens."

"Deal!" Jenny agreed.

Petunia had tucked in a couple of plates along with the food. Jenny unwrapped their sandwiches and placed them on the plates. She pulled off the plastic wrap over the pickle spears and tore open the packet of chips. She presented the plate of food to Adam with a flourish.

"Something's different about the chicken salad today," he said appreciatively.

"I got some fresh tarragon from the inn's garden," Jenny told him. "And I added some blanched almonds for crunch."

"You're a sight for sore eyes, Jenny," Adam said, staring deep into her eyes.

Jenny took a dainty bite of her own sandwich and asked after the twins.

"Up to no good," Adam cribbed, shaking his head. "They are taking a boat out to one of the islands this weekend. Nick's bringing a friend along."

"Nick's coming here this weekend?" Jenny asked eagerly. "He hasn't returned my calls, the scamp."

Jenny rubbed the tiny gold heart hanging around her neck. She looked forward to seeing her son in a couple of days.

"Ready for cake?" she asked Adam.

"Is that the special chocolate cake?" Adam asked. "The same one you made for Asher Cohen?"

"It's not the same cake," Jenny said. "Just the same recipe."

"Asher Cohen was supposed to have exacting standards. If he asked for this cake, it must be something special."

"Just because he asked for this cake?" Jenny pouted.

"Anything you cook is exceptional, Jenny," Adam praised. "You already know that."

"Doesn't hurt to get a compliment."

They bantered over the generous slices of cake until they could eat no more.

"I'm saving this for later," Adam said, licking his lips. "Any more of this and I'll fall asleep on my desk."

"Not so soon," Jenny warned. "You promised to hear me out."

"Shoot!" Adam said.

"There's no doubt that Asher Cohen was murdered, right?"

Adam nodded. He couldn't keep that from Jenny any longer.

"The most obvious suspect is always the spouse, right?" Jenny began. "That brings us to Linda. Linda Cohen was a trophy wife when they got married. She's what, almost thirty years younger than Asher. That makes her about 70 now."

"Correct," Adam said.

"She seems to have loved her husband. There are two things in her favor. She was right there in front of me during the parade. And she was still there when they were handing out the awards. The main thing we can't ignore … she's immobile."

"She could still have hired someone for the job,"

Adam said, playing devil's advocate.

"Why would she do that? There's no motive."

"Maybe she fell out of love with the old man," Adam mused.

"Of course!" Jenny cried with sarcasm. "That must be it. She fell in love with someone else and wanted the old man out of the way."

"It's been known to happen," Adam said seriously.

"You have to admit that's farfetched," Jenny argued.

"Possible, but not probable," Adam conceded.

"Hans Geller," Jenny said next. "He can't do anything right. He's belligerent and he's a mean drunk. He was disgruntled about a lot of things."

"Did he have anything against Asher?"

"Most of his ire seems to be directed at Luke Stone," Jenny explained. "Luke says Asher was calling the shots, but Hans didn't know that. Luke was the bad guy as far as Hans is concerned."

"Maybe Hans found out his grandpa wasn't too happy with him."

"So he gassed a 100 year old man?" Jenny asked. "I

don't think he's that industrious. He might have done something physical in a fit of temper but…"

"You said he's always drunk," Adam prompted. "He may not have been in his senses when he did it."

"Could be," Jenny agreed. "Hans is lying about a lot of stuff. He told me he's leaving town for good. He has no interest in Cohen Construction. But the opposite is true, apparently."

"Yeah?"

"Luke told me Hans hopes to inherit. He wants to take over Cohen Construction. Sit in a fancy office and call the shots."

"He might feel entitled," Adam pointed out. "He's the blood relative, after all, not Luke Stone."

"I did get that impression," Jenny nodded. "Another thing, he has no alibi. He was out picking up booze for the party. But no one can vouch for that. He could have been anywhere. Maybe he was in the back alley where Asher parked his truck."

"You seem to have talked to a lot of people," Adam admitted grudgingly. "When do you find the time to do it, Jenny?"

"Stop distracting me, Sheriff," Jenny snapped. "We are not done yet."

"Okay," Adam relented. "Who's next?"

"Luke Stone," Jenny said. "He's poured his blood and sweat into Cohen Construction. Linda says he was like a son to Asher."

"What would be his motive?"

"He hated Asher!"

Adam sat up with a jerk.

"How do you know that?"

"He told me himself."

Adam's face fell.

"Probably doesn't mean anything. A killer doesn't go around announcing he hated his victim."

"I thought so too," Jenny agreed. "But Luke doesn't have an alibi either. He was out of town picking up lumber."

"He told us that too," Adam said. "We are trying to get in touch with the man he met."

"So none of this is news to you?" Jenny asked Adam.

She had been on a roll but now she felt deflated.

"The police have been working on this case just like

you have, Jenny. It's our job."

"You're right," she said softly.

"We are here to talk about what you found out," Adam reminded her. "Why don't you go on?"

"Luke and Hans are at loggerheads. Luke found Hans drinking on the job and banned him from using any tools or working on site. Hans is not happy about it."

"Does Luke hope to inherit the business?" Adam asked.

"Negative," Jenny said. "He seems keen on retirement."

"So you don't think he had a motive?"

"Other than hating Asher … none."

"He may have hated the old man," Adam said. "I doubt he acted on it."

"That makes Luke a weak suspect," Jenny said with frustration.

"What about the other kids?"

"I talked to some of them," Jenny told Adam. "They are a peculiar lot, I can tell you."

"I think they are all senile," Adam muttered.

"Two of Linda's kids didn't come here for the centennial."

"I know Ryan well," Adam told her. "We joined the army at the same time."

"I haven't met the youngest daughter yet," Jenny told him.

"Tell me about the older ones," Adam prompted.

"Walt, the oldest, didn't seem very close to Asher. The same goes for his sister Emma. There's another one called Heidi who hated him. I didn't ask any of these for their alibis. They have barely visited Pelican Cove over the years. They just came here for the centennial. They are well off and leading comfortable lives elsewhere."

"So you talked to all the Cohens," Adam observed. "Can't say I've done that myself."

"There's one more guy," Jenny remembered. "Linda's son-in-law. He's always in need of more money according to Luke."

"That's Todd Buckler," Adam noted. "He seemed quite subdued when I talked to him. He has a farm in Maryland."

"I need to talk to him," Jenny said.

She waited for Adam to say something. Adam leaned back in his chair and closed his eyes. He seemed to be going over all the information.

"So?" Jenny prompted impatiently. "What do you think?"

"You've been thorough, Jenny," Adam admitted grudgingly. "I think you know almost as much as we do."

"Almost? So there's something I don't know about all this?"

"There are some things I am not allowed to disclose," Adam said. "You know that."

"Of course," Jenny bristled. "This is an ongoing investigation and you cannot comment on it."

"Right," Adam said. "I don't make the rules, Jenny."

"None of these people have a strong motive," Jenny wailed. "Do you agree with that opinion?"

"I suppose it's safe to say that."

"We have to be missing something, Adam."

"Why don't you give it a rest?" Adam suggested. "Take a day off from this. Do something fun."

"Like what? Take a boat out on the water?"

"I was about to suggest that," Adam said eagerly. "But I guess you will say no."

"Your guess is right," Jenny said, standing up.

"I don't care what we do, as long as we can spend some time together."

"We just did that," Jenny protested.

"Not like this," Adam said, his deep blue eyes boring into hers. "Somewhere private, away from prying eyes."

Jenny's heart raced as she thought of a witty response. But her mind failed her. She turned around on her heel and walked out of Adam's office, fanning her flaming cheeks.

Chapter 12

Jimmy Parsons sat on the beach outside his little cabin, staring at the ocean. He hadn't slept a wink in three days. His splitting headache made coherent thought impossible. His hand shook as he shielded his eyes and stared out over the shimmering sand. The sun was playing games with him. Or maybe it was his mind. He thought he saw something bobbing in the water. Was it something, or someone? A peculiar song traveled over the waves, drawing him to them. Was he seeing a mermaid in broad daylight?

Jimmy knew what he must do. Star had been pretty clear on that. He went inside and showered and put on some clean clothes. Before the sauce got him, Jimmy had been a man of his word. He tried to summon the inner strength that had helped him through tough situations.

Star was drinking iced coffee on the deck of the Boardwalk Café, listening to the Magnolias chatter around her. She was thinking of Jimmy. Had she been too harsh with him? She knew it wasn't just a matter of will power. His condition was far beyond that. She vowed to be extra nice to him.

"Where are you lost?" Jenny nudged her. "I've called out your name three times."

"Just thinking about work," Star said. "I have to go."

She walked back to her gallery, wondering if she was too old to attempt a relationship.

Jenny spotted a missed call on her phone when she finally sat down for lunch.

"Linda called," she said aloud. "I wonder what she wants."

"Why don't you take off after lunch?" Petunia asked. "You can visit Linda if you want to."

Jenny was glad of the generous offer. Her days were running together. The café was proving to be a test of her endurance. She had never had to work so hard in her life before. But she loved every minute of it.

"Thanks. I think I will take you up on that."

"What's new in the crab salad today?"

"I added some sliced black olives with the sweet peppers," Jenny told her. "Just enough to add a salty touch."

"The customers loved it, obviously," Petunia said, looking pleased. "We had barely enough left for our lunch."

"Captain Charlie liked it too," Jenny nodded, referring

to her favorite customer. "He wants me to prepare a big batch just for him."

"Do you think we should start selling this in containers?" Petunia asked thoughtfully. "Customers can eat it any way they like then, maybe have a picnic on the beach."

They discussed the merits of the idea for a while. Jenny helped Petunia clean up the kitchen and set off for the Cohen estate.

Linda Cohen was seated in her usual spot by the window, looking out at the ocean. Jason Stone lounged on a small sofa.

"I didn't expect to see you here, Jason!" Jenny exclaimed.

"I needed Linda's signature on some stuff. I should get going."

"Stay," Jenny said.

She wanted to say more but she held herself back because of Linda.

"How are you, Jenny?" Linda asked.

"I meant to call you today," Jenny hastened to explain.

"I called you here for a reason," Linda said. "Jason is

reading the will later this evening. I want you to be present."

"Isn't that private?" Jenny asked.

"I will have to give you the details later anyway," Linda said. "It's best you stick around for it."

Jenny liked the idea. She could observe everyone's reactions first hand.

"Do you know what to expect from it?" she asked Linda. "Did Asher tell you, I mean."

"I have an idea," she said. "But he went to meet Jason last week. He refused to tell me why. He might have changed his will at that time."

She looked at Jason expectantly.

"I can't comment on that," Jason said firmly.

"We'll know soon enough," Linda said. "Why don't you hang around until then? Ring for some food if you are hungry."

"I just had lunch," Jenny assured her.

"Do you want to check out our pool?" Linda asked generously. "It's a work of art. We have extra swimsuits for guests. You can borrow one if you like."

It was a scorching summer day. Jenny felt the sweat pool under her armpits and was tempted.

"I might take you up on that."

"Take care of her, Jason," Linda ordered. "I'm going to take a nap."

Jenny hadn't met Jason since their fateful dinner at Ethan's. She felt a bit uncomfortable, talking about something personal in the Cohens' home.

Jason beat her to it.

"I wanted to apologize, Jenny," he said sincerely. "I wasn't thinking straight."

"It's my fault too," she said. "I guess I was tired."

"You are overworked," Jason shot back immediately.

Then he backed down again.

"I'm sorry again. I didn't mean to presume."

"Don't be so formal," Jenny said softly. "We're good. There's nothing to worry about."

"How does that swim sound?" Jason asked with a grin.

"Tempting," Jenny smiled.

"Let's go, then," Jason said, pulling her to her feet.

"We have plenty of time."

"I was hoping to meet Linda's son-in-law."

"I saw him drive out with Dawn. But they should be back soon."

Jenny trudged through the big house, hand in hand with Jason. He showed her the assortment of swimwear she could choose from and left her to change. They met at the pool. Jenny felt a bit nervous about facing Jason in a swimsuit. She just hoped he liked a woman with curves, and a scar or two.

Blue and white striped cabanas were set up by the poolside. Jenny spotted a familiar trio of women. Emma and Heidi were lounging in the chairs, their faces shielded by large straw hats. Walter was mixing some drinks at a bar. A man and a woman she hadn't seen before were in the water, frolicking with a little girl.

Jenny dipped a toe in the water to check the temperature. It was cool but not too cold. She sat down on the edge and jumped in.

"This is wonderful," she squealed.

"Isn't it?" Jason asked.

He had made a perfect shallow dive into the water.

"Who are those people?" Jenny asked, tipping her head at the new couple.

"Maria and Paul," Jason told her. "They came here for the reading of the will."

"Are Linda's sons coming?"

"They both have extenuating circumstances," Jason explained. "I'm going to go ahead without them."

"What about Asher's funeral?"

"He was cremated," Jason told her. "He didn't want a funeral or memorial or whatever. There will be no obituary in the paper either. Those were his final wishes."

Jenny floated on her back for a while, taking deep breaths. She swam a few laps along the breadth of the pool and reminded herself to thank Linda for this rare treat. She hadn't felt so refreshed in days.

Another couple came out, dressed for the pool. The woman was younger than Jenny but looked a bit frumpy. Jenny spotted some gray roots at her temples. The man with her was average in looks and personality. He had a square jaw and a bovine expression. He was biting his nails, looking around for something or someone. The little girl screamed when she saw the new couple and swam toward them.

"That's Todd Buckler," Jason gasped, swimming up to Jenny. "That's Linda's son-in-law."

"Is that her daughter with him?" Jenny asked, trying not to stare at them.

"That's Dawn," Jason confirmed, "my cousin."

"She may be the youngest, but she looks a little worse for wear."

"She has a hard life," Jason said. "Give her a chance and she'll tell you all about it herself."

Emma and Heidi were sitting up in their chairs and looking at Jenny. Emma gave her a friendly wave.

"I need to talk to Todd," she said, climbing out of the pool.

She showered and dressed and came back out, hoping she hadn't missed the elusive man. He was the one member of the Cohen family she hadn't talked to yet.

Todd was sprawled in a deck chair, watching his wife and daughter swim. Jenny introduced herself.

"I'm a friend of Linda's."

"I know who you are," Todd smirked. "Emma just told me."

"Do you have time for a quick chat?"

"I'm not a Cohen," he said.

"No, but your wife is. You are closely related to them."

"Whaddaya want to know?"

"Tell me something about Asher."

"Not much to tell. He was crazy about that business of his."

"You mean he worked too much?"

"A man's gotta sit back some time. Let the kids take over."

"Were you interested in working at Cohen Construction?" Jenny asked curiously.

None of the others had hinted at that.

"Not me," Todd denied immediately. "I've got my own farm up in Maryland. It keeps me busy."

"Do you enjoy being a farmer?"

"It's what my family does. My Pa did it before me. I promised him I wouldn't give the farm up. Dawn and I make a good team."

"Your wife works on the farm too?"

"There's a lot to be done," Todd nodded. "There's the animals – the pigs and the chickens – there's cows and sheep to be milked, cream to be churned, cheese to be made."

"So you live on a homestead?"

"That's right," Todd said proudly. "We're doing great. I've got big plans for us."

"Were you here for the centennial?"

"Sure was. Dawn came here a week before that with our little girl but I couldn't leave the farm for that long. I drove up on the morning of the 4th."

"Were you here for the parade?"

"I helped decorate that truck," Todd boasted. "Almost got up there with Asher. But my girl scraped her knee and started making a fuss. I was standing in the crowd by the side of the road."

"Were you with Linda?"

"Somewhere around her," Todd said. "What's with all the questions, lady?"

"Oh, I'm just trying to get an idea of where everyone was. Funny you mention Linda. I was standing near her and I don't remember seeing you at the awards ceremony."

Todd seemed annoyed. Then his face cleared and he smiled.

"Oh right. I told you my baby girl was crying? I went to get her some ice cream. She has to have one when she gets a boo-boo."

"Do you know if Asher had any enemies?"

Todd shrugged.

"I couldn't tell you that. I don't live here, you see. Maybe you should ask Hans, or Luke."

"You know Luke?"

"Of course I do. He's my wife's uncle."

"Oh, yeah…"

"Are we done here?" Todd asked. "I want to take a dip before we go in."

"Last question," Jenny said. "Did you see Asher argue with anyone?"

"Nope," he said. "Look, you want to know what I think? He was old. He just got tired of living. He took the easy way out."

"You're saying he took his own life?"

"That's right," Todd said. "I have to go now."

He stood up and gave a whoop before jumping into the water. Jenny stepped back just in time to avoid getting wet.

"What do you think?" Jason asked.

He was naked from the waist up, wearing his trousers. He looked at her quizzically as he toweled his head dry. Jenny tried not to stare at him.

"He didn't say much. He thinks Asher committed suicide."

Jason let out a snort.

"He's messing with you. Everyone knows what happened to Asher."

"He doesn't have an alibi."

"Let's discuss this later," Jason said. "It's time to go in."

Jenny followed Jason into the house. She waited outside a dressing room for him. He led her to a big room which was obviously the library. Like every other room in the house, it was lavishly decorated. Wooden bookshelves soared from floor to ceiling, stacked with a variety of books. A large rectangular table graced the center of the room, surrounded by chairs upholstered in green leather.

Walt, Emma and Heidi were already seated at the table. A tea had been laid out with three tiered stands of sandwiches and cakes. A maid wheeled Linda into the room.

Todd walked in with Dawn, followed by Maria and Paul.

"I think we are ready to begin," Jason said, nodding at everyone.

Chapter 13

Jenny sat out on the deck with a tall frosty glass of coffee in front of her. She had started churning out her own version of frappes and the tourists were lapping them up. She had never allowed herself the indulgence, until now.

She had sent Petunia home early for a change. The mercury had crossed the hundred degree mark and it had taken a toll on the older lady. The café was closed for the day but some people lingered on the deck, enjoying the ocean view. Jenny didn't mind them. She had work to do.

She pulled out a writing pad from her bag, along with some colored pens and sticky notes. She started noting down everything she knew about Asher Cohen and his life. She had her big epiphany an hour later.

She had been focusing on his life in Pelican Cove and his family. What if what happened to him was connected to his past? The past he didn't like to talk about?

She needed her laptop for any more research. It was time to head home. She walked to Williams Seafood Market. It was her turn to pick up fresh fish for their dinner. Chris was at the checkout desk as usual. He perked up when he saw Jenny.

"What's good today?" she asked him.

"Soft shell crabs are in season. They are really easy to cook. Just dredge them in some seasoned flour and fry them."

Jenny knew her son Nick hadn't tried them yet. They were a local delicacy in the Chesapeake area so she decided to try out some recipes using them.

"Give me half a dozen of those," she nodded. "A pound of jumbo shrimp and four fillets of sea bass, please."

"You expecting some company?" Chris asked casually as he packed her purchases.

"Never hurts to have extra," she said. "Nick might come in tomorrow."

She rubbed the tiny golden charm around her neck, deciding she needed to talk to her son that night.

"How's Heather? Getting ready for her big date?"

Jenny felt uncomfortable talking about it.

"She told you about Duster, huh?"

Chris shrugged noncommittally. His lips stretched into

a terse smile.

"She wants to sow her wild oats, let her."

"Are you really fine with this?" Jenny asked with concern. "You don't need to put up a show for me, Chris. We are friends too. You can tell me anything."

"I'm trying to keep it together," he admitted. "What choice do I have?"

"Don't you want to try dating someone else?"

Chris Williams shook his head.

"Heather has always been the only one for me. There's not a single doubt in my mind."

"Bravo!" Jenny applauded. "You're the bigger person, then."

"I don't care about that," Chris told her. "Let her have her way."

Jenny walked home, thinking about how she would cook the soft shell crabs. Star and Jimmy Parsons were sitting out on the porch. Jimmy looked a bit pale. Jenny wondered what was wrong with him. He even looked like he had lost some weight.

Jenny cooked dinner and spent some time with her aunt and Jimmy.

"I need to check on something," she told them after the dishes had been cleared. "You will have to excuse me."

"Jimmy and I are going to watch an old movie," Star said. "Don't mind us."

Jenny went to her room and hooked up her laptop. She began running some basic searches about the war. She put special emphasis on Germany before and during the war. The stories she read brought tears to her eyes. Finally, she could take it no more. She flung the laptop aside and rushed outside. She needed some air.

"Going for a walk?" Star called out. "Don't stay out too long."

Star always said that to her, just like she had when Jenny was a teenager. It was something they joked about often. Jenny couldn't summon a smile. She waved at her aunt and shut the door of the tiny cottage.

Roses bloomed at Seaview, perfuming the air with their heady fragrance. The lights came on when Jenny neared the big three storey house. She stared up at it, unable to believe it belonged to her. She wondered how long it would be before she could move in.

Terrible images flashed before Jenny's eyes as she walked on the beach. She shivered as she tried to assimilate everything she had just read. She barely noticed when a hairy body came bounding toward her and almost struck her down.

"Tank," she said weakly.

The yellow Labrador ran in circles around her, his tail wagging frantically. Adam Hopkins walked up, leaning heavily on his stick. Jenny noticed he was back to using his stick a lot again. She refrained from asking if he had had a relapse.

"Hey, Jenny," he greeted her. "You look a bit preoccupied."

"I've been thinking," she nodded.

She felt a lump in her throat and couldn't continue. Would Adam believe her theory? Would anyone?

A pair of strong arms came around her and held her close.

"What's the matter?" Adam asked, alarmed. "Something wrong? Is Nick alright?"

She pulled herself together.

"Nick must be fine. In fact, I need to call him tonight. Thanks for reminding me."

"You're working too hard," Adam noted. "What about the kids Petunia hired to help you out? Haven't you put them to work yet?"

"Those kids are helping a lot," Jenny said. "I'm fine. It's just…"

"Just what?"

Jenny patted Tank and scratched him below his ears. He whimpered and nuzzled her. Adam took the hint and said nothing. They walked on for some time and turned around.

"How's the investigation going?" Adam asked her.

Jenny's face finally broke into a smile.

"I should ask you that."

"You know I can't tell you anything," Adam said. "But nothing's stopping you from sharing your thoughts."

"You just want to pick my brain so you can take all the credit."

"Correct," Adam said.

They both laughed at that.

"I may be on to something," Jenny admitted. "But I'm not ready to talk about it yet."

"Jason told me you were present at the reading of the will."

"I was. But if my latest theory means anything, we won't have to worry about the will."

"Now you've done it," Adam groaned. "I'm going to stay up all night thinking about that."

"I thought you stay up thinking about me," Jenny teased.

"That too," Adam said, giving her a scorching look.

They sat in the sand with Seaview at their back and the ocean before them. The whitecaps sparkled in the dark and the gently lapping waves of the low tide finally relaxed Jenny. They talked about every topic on earth for what seemed like hours. Jenny had never felt closer to Adam.

Jimmy Parsons came out on the porch, followed by Star. He swooped down for a quick kiss. Jenny saw Star pat him on the back and wondered what was going on between the older couple.

"Are you ready to come in, Jenny?" Star called out.

Adam stood up.

"Duty starts at 7 AM tomorrow. I know your day begins much before that."

Tank stood up reluctantly and they walked slowly away from Jenny.

Star had put the kettle on in the kitchen.

"I could use some herbal tea," she told Jenny. "I'm too wound up."

"What's wrong?" Jenny asked with concern. "Is it Jimmy? You seem to be getting along fine."

"Jimmy joined a support group," she said. "He's trying to stop drinking."

"That's wonderful!" Jenny exclaimed. "Did you ask him to do it?"

Star shook her head.

"He's tried it before. Obviously, it didn't work. I didn't want to pressure him."

"So he's doing it on his own?" Jenny smiled. "That's good. It means he's motivated."

"It's hard on him," Star explained. "He's going through withdrawal. He won't talk about it but I can see the signs."

"Your support means a lot to him, I'm sure."

Star was feeling emotional. Jenny talked to her for some time, trying to distract her. The phone rang. It was Nick, Jenny's son.

"When are you getting here?" she burst out. "Rumor is you are spending the weekend in Pelican Cove."

"That's right, Mom. I should be there by ten. Depends on how soon I start from here. The twins and I are taking a boat out."

"I was thinking, maybe we could do something together?"

She talked to Nick for a while and gave him all her typical motherly instructions. Her eyes closed before her head hit the pillow.

Captain Charlie was first in line at the café the next morning.

"Linda said you are looking into who killed Asher," he said, picking up his coffee. "I know you'll do a better job than the cops, just like last time."

Jenny blushed at the praise, then remembered something Captain Charlie had said to her.

"How well did you know Asher, Captain Charlie?"

"He was always around, ever since I was a little boy."

"Did you ever hang out with him?"

Captain Charlie nodded.

"Took him deep sea fishing in the season. I know all the good spots, see? He owned a couple of boats but he wanted me to take them out."

"Can you tell me something about him?"

"Wasn't much of a talker," Captain Charlie grumbled. "Stuck to the same routine year after year. Talked about his kids a lot though. Wanted them to come visit more often."

"Did he tell a lot of war stories?"

"No Sir! Any talk of war was off limits. I asked him about his ocean crossing once. Didn't go down too well."

"Must be a painful subject," Jenny murmured.

"You're right, Jenny. Talking about it would only bring it all back. And I'm sure he didn't want that."

Nick rushed in at 9:30 and swept Jenny into a hug.

"How'd you get here so early? I told you not to speed, Nicky!"

"Relax, Mom," he said, picking up a hot muffin off a tray. "It's just a three hour drive. I started early."

"What are your plans? I don't suppose you're going to spend the day talking to your mother?"

"The twins are waiting outside," he said. "Can you pack some lunch for us, please? We can have dinner together, promise! Adam and the twins will come too."

Nick gave her a Cliff Notes version of how he was faring at his internship. He grabbed the lunch basket Jenny handed over and rushed out.

The Magnolias sailed in after that. Heather was wearing a new yellow frock with white daisies on it. Molly was dressed in lime green Capri pants and a white sleeveless top. She looked a bit awkward in her new clothes.

"How do we look?" Heather asked as she pirouetted before Jenny.

Jenny slapped her forehead as her mouth dropped open.

"That's right! You're going to meet Buster."

"Duster, Jenny!" Heather said with a pout. "We are all set to go to their beach house."

"You'll be careful, won't you?" she asked, looking uncertainly at Molly.

"Yes, Mother, we will!" Heather teased.

"I don't feel so good," Molly stuttered. "Maybe you should go on your own, Heather."

"No way," Heather warned. "You promised, Molly."

"Are you sure they are expecting me?"

"Duster's cousin is an English professor in a community college up north. You'll get along just fine."

Molly relaxed visibly at the mention of a professor.

"Let's go then," she said. "We don't want to be late."

"Can we have two iced coffees to go please?" Heather asked.

"What about Betty Sue?" Jenny asked.

"She thinks I am taking Molly shopping."

"You need to come clean," Jenny warned. "You're not a teenager, Heather."

"My grandma will never get behind this," Heather said emphatically. "I don't have a choice."

"Don't do anything rash, okay?"

"Says the woman who's dating two guys at once," Heather shot back.

Chapter 14

"Are there many Jewish people in Pelican Cove?" Jenny asked Betty Sue Morse, placing a tall glass of iced coffee before her.

Betty Sue dropped her knitting and cursed out loud.

"Huh, what?"

"You know the Cohens are Jewish, right?" Jenny asked. "How many other Jewish families do we have in Pelican Cove?"

"Not too many," Betty Sue told her. "Why?"

"I have a hunch."

"Does it have anything to do with Asher?" Betty Sue asked.

"I think so," Jenny said. "Can you give me some information about these people? Where can I find them?"

Molly looked up from the book she had been reading.

"My mother knows a Jewish family. They moved here around the same time my Grandma did."

"That's all?" Jenny asked.

"There's a lack of new blood in Pelican Cove," Betty Sue lamented. "The refugees came here after the great storm of 1962. Hardly any new families have come here since then. Kids grow up and move to the city. Very few come back like my Heather did."

"Towns up north have larger Jewish communities," Star explained. "They have a synagogue too. We don't."

"What's with the sudden interest in Jewish people, Jenny?" Heather asked.

"I want to know more about their life here," Jenny said. "I'm especially interested in talking to families of Holocaust survivors."

"I see where you're going with this," Star said thoughtfully, "but I'm not sure why."

"Like I said," Jenny said casually, "it's just a hunch."

Adam Hopkins came into the café at noon. He ordered the lunch special and sat at a table out on the deck.

"Slacking off?" Jenny asked him.

Adam rarely took time off for lunch.

"I'm not getting anywhere with this Cohen murder. I thought a change of scene might give me some new ideas."

"Why don't you talk to me?" Jenny quipped. "I may have a couple of thoughts on the subject."

"I like to proceed in a methodical manner, Jenny. I am in the process of verifying everyone's alibis."

"Don't forget to look for a motive," Jenny teased.

Molly called in with some information about the Jewish family her mother knew. She promised to go with Jenny to meet them.

Jenny, Molly and Heather gathered at the Rusty Anchor later that evening.

"What's all this about?" Heather asked. "Why did you want to meet these people?"

"I was surprised at the questions you asked them," Molly said.

"No one talks about Asher's life before he came to Pelican Cove. But I think it could have a connection with what happened to him. I want to find out more about his prior life."

"Did talking to my mother's friends help?" Molly asked.

"I didn't want to miss that," Heather complained. "Why didn't you take me along?"

"We can tell you about it now," Molly consoled her.

Eddie Cotton came over with their drinks.

"One of my best customer's gone sober," he whined. "At least I still got him."

Jenny looked at where he was pointing. Hans Geller was seated at the bar, nursing a beer. He looked a bit worse for wear.

"You were saying?" Heather prodded her.

"I didn't find out much," she said glumly. "The people we met are the only Jewish family in Pelican Cove other than the Cohens. Another couple moved a few miles north to a town that has a synagogue. Asher Cohen wasn't very religious, it seems. He didn't really hang out with other Jewish folks."

"You think he was trying to hide his Jewish heritage?" Heather asked.

Jenny thought for a while.

"Hard to say, Heather. Some people are just not devout."

"Were these people Holocaust Survivors too?"

"No. Their grandparents came to America at the turn of the twentieth century."

"What difference does it make?" Molly asked.

"I have this theory..." Jenny hesitated.

"Spit it out," Heather said. "What's with all the suspense."

"What if Asher was targeted because he was a Jew?"

"You mean this was a hate crime?" Molly asked. "What made you think of that?"

"It's been known to happen," Jenny said meekly. "Hate crimes have been on the rise since the last couple of years. I read about it online."

"What does Adam say about this?" Heather asked.

"I haven't talked to him about it," Jenny admitted.

The girls chatted for a while. Jenny walked home after that, lost in thought. Star and Jimmy Parsons were waiting for her at home. Star had cooked a roast for dinner but Jenny barely tasted it. She went to her room and collapsed on the bed. Her mind was teeming with all the information she had found online.

An hour later, Jenny abandoned any thoughts of an early night. She splashed water on her face and stepped outside. Star and Jimmy were sitting on the porch, reminiscing about the summer of 1994.

Jenny didn't stop to smell the roses at Seaview. She walked away from the cottage at a grueling pace, secretly hoping to run into Adam. She found him sitting in the sand a few minutes later, Tank by his side. She flopped down next to him.

"Something wrong?" she asked him.

It was Adam's wedding anniversary. He realized he hadn't thought about his dead wife in a while. Had he moved on?

Adam felt a surge of affection when he looked at Jenny, followed by guilt. He shook his head and stared out at the sea.

"Do you know the demographics of Pelican Cove?" she asked him.

"There's a shortage of women," Adam teased. "Especially beautiful women like you."

Jenny felt her cheeks burn.

"I was thinking more on the lines of racial makeup."

"We don't have a lot of diversity here, Jenny. You must have observed that by now."

"That's an understatement," Jenny stressed. "Did you know there's only one Jewish family in town other than the Cohens?"

Adam cleared his throat.

"Actually, I thought the Cohens were the only one."

"What if Asher paid a price for that?"

"How so?" Adam asked, sitting up straighter.

"What if he was targeted because he was a Jew?"

"You are saying this was a hate crime?" Adam asked skeptically. "That's a big leap, Jenny."

"Not really," she mumbled. "It's a strong motive."

"There are plenty of other strong motives," Adam argued. "Greed? Hatred? Revenge?"

"I talked to almost everyone connected to Asher," Jenny said. "I don't think any of these motives apply."

"I disagree," Adam said. "You'll see."

"What does that mean?" Jenny asked. "Are you planning to make an arrest?"

"I can't tell you that. But you're way off base with that hate crime theory."

Jenny discussed her theory with Star later that night. Jimmy had just bid them goodnight. He was looking like a different person these days.

"Don't you agree with me?" Jenny asked her aunt after she told her about her theory.

"You need more information about this," Star said thoughtfully. "And for that, you need to talk to more people. I think I may have something for you. I need to check something with Jimmy first though."

"Are you and Jimmy an item now?" Jenny asked slyly. "He's spending a lot of time here."

"Jimmy's a friend," Star said simply. "I'm just being there for him. I don't think he needs any more complications now. Trying to kick the habit is hard enough."

"You're a gem of a person, Aunt!" Jenny said, hugging her impulsively.

Star hurried up the steps of the Boardwalk Café the next morning. She was wearing her signature paint splattered smock. A few dirty paint brushes were peeping out of the front pocket.

The Magnolias were already seated on the deck, busy gossiping about the tourists.

"Got a minute, Jenny?" Star said as she accepted a glass of iced coffee.

"Sure. What's up?"

"You remember Jimmy has a few cottages on the island?"

"How can I forget?" Jenny rolled her eyes. "I took him for a beach bum and turns out he's quite the entrepreneur. I have never felt more foolish in my life."

"Jimmy didn't lift a finger to earn them," Betty Sue said, her hands poised over her knitting needles. "The Parsons have owned them for generations."

"Hush, Betty Sue!" Star snapped.

She looked at Jenny, trying to recapture her attention.

"There's a fellow renting one of those cottages. He's a professor in some college. He's here to study birds."

"And?" Jenny prompted.

"I think you want to talk to him."

Jenny caught on after a minute.

"Oh? That sounds great. Where do I find this person?"

"He takes a boat out in the marshes on most days," Star said. "Jimmy convinced him to come here for lunch today."

"I'll be waiting for him," Jenny said seriously.

"Who is this man?" Betty Sue demanded. "Why don't you tell us more?"

"Uh … why don't you let me talk to him first, Betty Sue?" Jenny asked. "I'll give everyone a full report tomorrow."

A short, thin man walked into the café at 1 PM. He wore a vest and a cap and held a pipe in his hand.

"No smoking in here," Petunia warned.

"Don't worry, this is not lit," he told her.

He walked over to the counter and looked around furtively.

"I'm here for my free lunch," he said. "Jimmy Parsons sent me."

Jenny caught on immediately.

"Welcome to the Boardwalk Café. What can I get you today?"

Jenny led the man to a cozy table near a window. She was back with his crab salad sandwich and sweet tea a few minutes later.

"Here you are," she said. "I'm Jenny King."

"Ira Brown," he introduced himself. "I've heard a lot

about the food here."

"Have you been here before?" Jenny asked.

"Oh no! I pack my own lunch. I don't believe in unnecessary expenses."

"This one's on the house," Jenny assured him. "I was hoping to ask you a few questions, Mr. Brown."

"I'm not ready to talk about my book yet," Ira Brown said uncertainly. "The Delmarva is home to some rare birds. You can read about them in my book."

"It's not about birds," Jenny hastened to explain. "It's about your culture."

Ira looked intrigued.

"I'm American, same as you are, I presume."

Jenny felt uncomfortable.

"Jimmy thought you were Jewish. I guess he was wrong."

Ira held up a hand while he chewed on his sandwich.

"I do come from a Jewish family. Or as you put it, I'm Jewish. What about it?"

"I recently read about the discrimination your people face in their everyday lives. Some accounts even mentioned abuse."

"My people don't have it easy," Ira said philosophically.

"How far would someone go to inflict harm?"

"You have heard of the Holocaust?" Ira asked.

He was warming up to the subject. Jenny detected a note of sarcasm in his question.

"Of course I have," she said quickly. "I was referring to current times."

"There is no limit to the hatred someone might feel. Neither is there a limit to the harm they can inflict."

"Could a person be killed for it?"

Ira answered simply.

"Yes."

Jenny felt her heart beat louder. Her instinct told her she was on the right track. She placed a piece of chocolate cake in front of Ira Brown and thanked him for his time.

Jenny wanted to sound her idea off someone. Adam had already told her what he thought of it. She decided to go see Jason. She walked to his office after the café closed, eager to learn his opinion of her theory.

Jason was rushing out when she reached his office.

"I have to go," he apologized. "Linda has just been arrested."

"I'm coming with you," Jenny stated, rushing after him.

Chapter 15

"Get out of here, Jenny," Adam snapped as soon as he saw her enter the police station. "This is none of your business."

"You know I'm helping Linda," she said, her hands on her hips. "I'm here to take care of her."

"Only her lawyer can do that," Adam warned. "Don't interfere."

"I'm her lawyer," Jason reminded him. "Can I go see her?"

Adam stepped aside reluctantly.

Linda Cohen was sitting in Adam's office. Jason hugged her and sat down beside her. That's when he noticed the wheelchair.

"Where's your wheelchair?" he exclaimed.

He whirled around and gave Adam a glare.

"What's going on, Sheriff? Have you stooped to harassing disabled people?"

Adam looked at Linda and quirked an eyebrow.

"Do you want to tell them, or should I?"

Linda's face barely showed any emotion.

"I don't need the wheelchair," she told them. "You know Asher hired a new therapist from Sweden? She worked wonders for me. I have been able to get up and get around on my own for a while now."

"What?" Jason's eyes popped out of their sockets. "Then why hide it?"

"That's what we want to know." Adam stood with his arms folded and feet apart in an aggressive stance.

"It was supposed to be a surprise," Linda explained. "Asher and I were going to cut his birthday cake together. I was going to stand right next to him in front of all our kids and guests."

"Linda didn't need an alibi because we all thought she couldn't get out of that wheelchair," Adam stated. "But this changes everything."

"How so?" Jenny demanded.

She had sneaked in behind Jason and had been listening to the drama unfold.

"She was right in front of me all the time during the parade."

"We know where Asher was during the parade," Adam dismissed. "He wasn't around when they were giving out the prizes. Neither was Linda."

Linda looked defiant but she said nothing.

"Do you deny it?" Adam asked her.

She shook her head.

"Can you tell us where you were?"

"It's private. I don't want to talk about it."

Jason stroked Linda's back and leaned forward to whisper in her ear.

"You don't have a choice."

"I don't care if you arrest me," Linda said stoically. "Some things are supposed to be a secret."

"You need to talk to your client," Adam told Jason. "You know how these things work."

Adam stepped out of his own cabin, giving Jason some time with his client.

"Who are you protecting, Linda?" Jenny asked. "Don't you realize how serious this is?"

Linda's eyes filled up with tears. Jason looked at her in alarm.

"What's the matter? Is it one of the kids?"

"I was with Asher," Linda blubbered. "In his car."

"What were you doing there?" Jason asked, aghast.

He looked at Jenny. This meant Linda was present at the scene of the crime. It didn't bode well for her.

Linda looked ashamed. Her eyes had a faraway look in them. She gave them a watery smile.

"I don't know how to say this."

"I'm your lawyer, Linda," Jason said patiently. "I need to know everything if I am to defend you. Jenny doesn't need to be here though."

He tipped his head at her. Jenny got the message and started to leave.

"No," Linda called out. "Stay."

She hesitated before turning red.

"Asher and I ... we were making out."

No one said a word.

"It was his birthday," Linda explained. "I owed him a kiss."

"What happened after you, err, kissed?" Jason asked.

"I walked back to the awards function," Linda said.

"Asher was going to park the truck and follow me."

"Why don't you tell this to Adam?" Jason pleaded. "It will make things easier."

"Don't you see?" Linda argued. "It was a private moment. The last thing I shared with my beloved Asher before he was taken from me."

"Let me see what I can do," Jason consoled her.

"I may have a lead," Jenny told Linda. "I'm going to try and get to the bottom of this, Linda. Don't worry."

Adam was talking to Nora, one of the clerks.

"You are wrong about Linda," Jenny told him. "What's her motive?"

"The spouse is always the most obvious suspect," Adam told her. "You know that."

"There's something else going on in this case."

"I know what your theory is," Adam told her. "It's too farfetched, Jenny. Surely you see that?"

"I think it's worth looking into," Jenny said stoutly before she stomped out.

Jenny walked to the seafood market, remembering she was supposed to get some fish for dinner. Chris greeted her.

"You seem preoccupied," he said. "Something wrong?"

Jenny shook her head and asked for her usual order.

"Did you like the soft shell crabs?" Chris asked her.

"Nick loved them," Jenny told him. "I'm going to grill them with barbecue sauce this time."

"Sounds yum," Chris laughed. "Anything you cook is tasty, Jenny. You have a gift."

"Say, Chris, do you know Dawn, Asher's youngest daughter?"

"Not very well. Why?"

"Was she in school with you?"

"She was a few years ahead of us. Didn't Heather tell you that?"

"Who did she hang out with? Do you know?"

Chris shrugged.

"Like I said, she was older than us. I have no idea."

Jenny had anticipated Jimmy would join them for dinner. She was right. Jimmy was displaying many interesting aspects of his personality now that he had stopped drinking.

"Did you meet that professor chap?" Jimmy asked her. "He's weird alright."

Jenny was stepping out for her walk when a luxury sedan pulled up outside Star's cottage. Jason Stone stepped out, looking exhausted. He undid the top button of his shirt and loosened his tie as he exhaled loudly.

"Have you had dinner?" Jenny asked him.

He shook his head.

Jenny went in and fixed a plate for Jason. She brought it out and handed it over to him.

"What happened?"

"They let her go," he said. "Linda wouldn't budge. Adam tried hard. But they didn't have enough to hold her there."

"How is she doing?"

"Linda's fine," Jason sighed. "She's a strong woman. She's sad though."

Jenny sat down next to Jason, lost in thought.

"How is it no one knows anything about Asher's life before he got here?"

"Some people block out bad memories," Jason said.

"He must have known other people in Germany."

Jason pursed his lips.

"Chances are, none of them made it here. His family didn't, as far as we know."

"He must have come in contact with other people? How about his time in Switzerland? Did he not meet anyone there? Or what about the ship that brought him here?"

"There might be records somewhere," Jason mused. "But they will be hard to find, Jenny. I'd say, impossible even."

"Do you know that for a fact?"

"Not really."

"I'm going to do some research," Jenny proclaimed.

"Research is always a good idea," Jason said. "I'm calling it a day now. I'm exhausted."

Jenny stifled a yawn and started walking on the beach. She needed the exercise, she told herself. She walked longer than usual without running into Adam. Reluctantly, she turned back and trudged home.

"What's this I hear about Linda Cohen?" Betty Sue asked the next day, twirling red wool over her needles. "Is it true, Jenny?"

"They let her go," Jenny replied.

"Have you followed the money trail?" Heather asked her. "What happens to the Asher estate? And who gets the business?"

"I forgot all about that," Jenny nodded. "All I know is everyone stands to gain something."

"Even the older kids?" Star asked.

"Yes, even Walter and Heidi."

"What about Luke Stone?" Betty Sue asked.

"Luke Stone gets to run the business for as long as he wants," Jenny explained. "He just has to follow some conditions."

"I bet they have to do with that no-good grandson," Betty Sue huffed.

Jenny didn't get a chance to work on her computer until later that day. She ran several different searches about the Holocaust. She was looking for support groups or societies where survivors might meet or come together.

She found message boards with discussions on various topics and got sidetracked. Finally, she started making a list of organizations in the area. She hoped someone there knew Asher personally or had at least heard about him.

"How about another trip to the city?" she asked Heather on the phone. "We haven't gone anywhere in a while."

"Is this for fun?" Heather asked cagily. "Or are you planning to squeeze in some sleuthing?"

"A bit of both?"

"Talk to Molly," Heather said. "I'm in."

"What are you hoping to find at these places?" Molly asked her.

"I don't know," Jenny admitted. "Think of it as a history lesson."

Linda was sitting in a wingback chair, looking out at the ocean when Jenny visited her.

"I got rid of the wheelchair," she told Jenny. "The kids are thrilled."

"Do you like to swim?" Jenny asked. "You have a lovely pool."

"Aquatics was part of my therapy," Linda told her. "I can't swim laps yet, but one day soon."

"You and Asher belonged to different faiths," Jenny began. "How did you handle that?"

Linda shrugged.

"Asher didn't believe in God. After all the atrocities he witnessed, he refused to believe there was one."

"This same God helped him get away," Jenny pointed out.

"That's one point of view," Linda agreed. "But Asher didn't think that."

"What about his religion?"

"He didn't talk much about it. He just wanted to be left alone. He worked hard to build a good life for himself and his family. Work was his religion."

"What did you think about all this?"

"I had a crush on Asher since I was fourteen. I fell madly in love with him."

Jenny remembered a time when she had been besotted

with someone.

"You couldn't care less about religion, I suppose?"

"That's right. When he asked my Daddy's permission to marry me, I couldn't be happier."

"What about the kids?"

"Olga was a devout Jew," Linda explained. "She observed all the traditions. She raised the kids in the Jewish faith. Asher let her do what she wanted."

"And your own kids?"

"When Ryan came along, we had been married for a while. I took him to church sometimes. When he got older, I told him his father was Jewish."

"Your family may not have been very religious," Jenny conceded. "But they still had the Cohen name. Did your kids ever face any discrimination because of it?"

Linda looked perturbed.

"I never gave it much thought. You will have to ask Dawn."

"Was Asher a member of any special organizations or societies?" Jenny asked.

"He was in the Rotary," Linda replied.

"I mean, any groups from his old country, or war survivors."

"Not to my knowledge," Linda said. "A couple of groups up north tried to woo him. They wanted him to come and talk about his experiences. One of them sent some kind of annual letter every year."

"Letter?" Jenny asked immediately. "What sort of letter? Do you have a copy?"

Linda shook her head.

"Asher threw them out. I think they provided updates on members. Births, deaths, bar mitzvahs, that kind of thing."

"Asher wasn't interested in socializing with other Jews, then."

"I guess you could say that," Linda shrugged. "I never gave it much thought."

Jenny wished Jason had accompanied her that day. She really felt like taking a dip in the big pool.

"Say you survive something terrible," Jenny asked Star over dinner. "You come out of an impossible situation. Would that make you believe in God or not?"

Star shrugged.

"You are assuming staying alive is a gift," Star said. "What if you lost everything that was dear to you? Every living hour would be a curse, then."

Chapter 16

Linda Cohen was called in for questioning again. Neither Jason nor Jenny could do anything about it. Jenny knew she needed to do more research to explore her own theory. She did something unprecedented and took a day off from the café.

Jenny shut herself in Star's cottage and switched off her phone. Her intense research on the Internet produced more questions than answers. But she knew what she needed to do.

"We are going to the city," she told Molly. "Plan to spend the whole day there."

"Don't worry," Molly assured her. "I can call in sick. The library will survive without me for one day."

"Grandma knows I am going with you," Heather told her.

"What are you planning to do exactly?" Molly asked.

"I am going to track down Asher Cohen," Jenny said resolutely.

The girls started off early, with Jenny anxious to spend as much time in the city as she could.

"So what is this place we are going to?" Heather asked.

"It's like a museum," Jenny admitted. "I am interested in their archives. I have an appointment with one of their experts."

"What does Adam say about all this?" Molly wondered.

"He doesn't know anything about our trip," Jenny fumed. "I prefer it that way."

"Why?"

"He shot my theory down the other day. I'd rather confront him with something concrete."

"Fingers crossed, then," Molly said.

"Don't get your hopes up though, Jenny," Heather warned. "It's still just a theory."

The building Jenny pulled up outside turned out to be much bigger than any of them had anticipated. They were directed to an usher who led them to a small office.

"Are you here for a family member?" the cheery young girl asked.

"Kind of," Jenny said. "Does it have to be anyone related to me?"

The girl shook her head and Jenny heaved a sigh of relief. She had debated getting some kind of letter from Linda but she wanted to get her hands on some actual information first.

"I see you requested some special help," the girl said. "Have you checked our online resources yet?"

"I ran some searches," Jenny nodded. "But I wasn't too successful."

"Okay. Please walk me through what you are looking for and what you have done so far."

Jenny explained her actions to the girl.

"The survivors' database is pretty accurate," the girl said. "Let me try a search again on my computer."

She looked up a couple of minutes later.

"You are sure Asher Cohen is the name? Do you know who might have added it here?"

Jenny didn't have an answer for that.

"Let me try something," the girl said. "Aha!" she exclaimed. "I was right. I guess there's always room for human error."

"What happened?" Jenny asked eagerly.

"Asher Cohen is in the victims' database. It looks like a data entry error."

"Can I find more information about him?" Jenny asked eagerly. "Where he is from, his family, or anything else you can find, really."

"We do that all the time," the girl smiled. "I can cross reference this name with our archives and see what I can come up with. Why don't you take a break? Have a coffee or something?"

Jenny thanked the girl and stepped outside, deep in thought. Molly and Heather were looking at the posters that hung in the hallway.

"Done already?" Molly asked.

Jenny explained what had happened.

"It's time for lunch anyway," Heather said, patting her stomach. "I saw a sign for a cafeteria."

The cafeteria surpassed their expectations. The girls all ordered side salads and a large veggie pizza.

"What are you thinking?" Molly asked Jenny, pouring creamy Caesar dressing over her salad.

"I feel numb. I am hoping that young girl finds something worthwhile."

Jenny knocked on the office door an hour later. Molly and Heather had decided to visit some of the exhibits.

"Come in," the girl called out eagerly. "You are in luck. I found a veritable treasure trove."

Jenny folded her hands in her lap and tried to sit still.

A small cardboard box lay on the table between them. The girl pulled out a faded book and a packet of old photos.

"This is an old journal depicting daily life," the girl told Jenny. "I'm afraid it's in German though. Can you read German?"

Jenny told her she could not.

"There are some news clippings leading up to the war," the girl went on. "There's a travel diary which is in English. And something you might appreciate most – photographs."

"Is Asher in those photos?" Jenny asked eagerly.

"I couldn't say," the girl grimaced. "But you can stay here and go through this material."

Jenny touched the papers gingerly, afraid she might damage them. She read the travel diary, her eyes filling up as she tried to imagine the plight of the writer. The photos intrigued her the most but she kept them for the last. She was almost reluctant to look at them. Her instincts told her she couldn't undo the information she found in them. She couldn't have been more right.

There were some group photos of people of different ages huddled together. Men, women and children with sordid expressions stared back at Jenny. Names were scrawled below the photos, identifying some of the people in the picture. Jenny marveled at the wealth of information available to her. She was holding history in her hands. A lot of that history was painful. Jenny couldn't help but wonder about the perseverance of the people who had overcome the worst kind of atrocities.

A curly haired stocky man of medium height could be seen in many of the photos. He had dark eyes and Jenny guessed them to be black or dark brown. Jenny's jaw dropped when she saw the name written below one of the photos. Asher Cohen. Jenny sat back, stunned.

Jenny was still trying to process what she had found when the girl got back.

"Did you find what you were looking for?" she asked.

"How long have you had this box?" she asked the girl.

"Let me check," the girl said. She tapped a few keys on the computer. "The material in this box has been donated over time, by more than one person. The earliest donation was in 1965."

"Do you know who did that?" Jenny asked.

"It's given right here at the bottom," the girl pointed out. "You are in luck. Not every donor leaves their information."

"Can I contact this person?" Jenny asked.

"No one's stopping you, I guess," the girl said. "Let's see, this address is in a suburb about twenty miles from here. And there's a phone number too."

Jenny felt her excitement ramp up.

"So I can call them and get an appointment if I want to meet them."

"Sure," the girl shrugged.

"How many people can access this information?" Jenny asked urgently.

"Anyone can access it," the girl explained. "Like you did."

"Can you tell me who saw this box before me?"

"Sorry. That's private."

Jenny rubbed the charm hanging around her neck and thought hard.

"Do you want to look at anything else?" the girl asked. "We close in half an hour but you can come back tomorrow."

Jenny thanked the girl for her help.

"I think I'm good for now."

She walked out in a daze and headed toward the parking lot. Heather and Molly were waiting for her by the car.

"Ready for some margaritas?" Heather squealed.

"Lead me on, girl!" Jenny muttered. "I need a giant frozen cocktail, something cold enough to give me brain freeze."

"Are you okay, Jenny?" Molly asked worriedly. "You look a bit weird."

"Wait till you hear what I found."

Jenny took them to her favorite Mexican restaurant in town. Piping hot tortilla chips arrived at their table along with a trio of salsas. They were followed by tall, generously salted frozen margaritas. Jenny munched some chips and drained half her drink, refusing to say much. Molly and Heather made small talk.

"What exactly did you find out, Jenny?" Heather asked finally.

Jenny told them about the box and all the photos and documents contained in it.

"None of this makes sense," Molly said, her eyes wide.

"You think?" Jenny scoffed. "If you ask me, we are dealing with a case of false identity."

"Huh?" Heather mumbled.

"Asher Cohen, our Asher, I mean, must have come across the actual Asher Cohen somewhere. He stole his papers and took his name."

"But why?" Molly and Heather chorused.

"Who knows?" Jenny flung her hands in the air.

"You've opened a can of worms," Molly said slowly.

"If our Asher is not Asher Cohen," Heather said, "then who is he? What is his name? Where did he come from? And why did he come to Pelican Cove?"

"I need to talk to Linda again," Jenny muttered.

"You think the Cohens know about this?" Heather asked.

"Hard to say," Jenny shrugged.

"What about Olga?" Molly asked. "His wife?"

"There is no account of an Olga Cohen," Jenny said flatly.

"But how can you be sure he's not our Asher?" Heather asked.

"I saw photos," Jenny said, leaning forward to pick up her drink. "He wasn't the same man."

"The Asher you saw was a hundred years old," Heather argued. "People look different as they age."

"You think I haven't considered that?" Jenny scoffed. "A man might lose height as he ages but he doesn't grow taller with age. And the man in the photo had a broken nose."

Heather opened her mouth.

"Don't tell me our Asher got plastic surgery! I'm sure it's not the same man."

"Isn't Asher Cohen a common name?" Molly asked.

"It is," Jenny agreed reluctantly.

"I have heard people added information about fellow prisoners or refugees," Molly said. "You think one of those people brought in those photos?"

"I am going to find out," Jenny told them. "Luckily, there's an address and phone number. We might have to make one more trip to the city."

"We can do that," Molly reassured her. "For now, just give it a rest, Jenny. Sleep on it."

"I'm getting the chicken fajitas," Heather nodded. "That's what you need. Some cheesy, spicy Mexican food that will stick to your ribs and put you in a food coma."

Jenny gave in.

The girls were so stuffed they could barely walk out of the restaurant.

"Told you that flan was too much," Jenny griped.

Molly and Heather coaxed her into watching a movie. Jenny admitted she had missed the whole movie theatre experience. Pelican Cove didn't have a cinema hall. Six months ago, she couldn't have imagined herself living in a place like that.

"Did you get that chimichanga recipe?" Heather asked her.

"I sure did," Jenny gloated. "I mean, I know how to make chimichangas. But the secret ingredient makes all the difference."

Molly and Heather kept their word. They didn't mention Asher Cohen at all. Jenny humored them and tried to have a good time.

Jimmy Parsons was sitting on the porch with Star when they got back home. His eyes were red and Jenny smelt a whiff of alcohol in the air.

"Jimmy had a drink today," Star told her later. "He was beating himself up about it."

"Does that mean he's out of the program?" Jenny asked.

Star shook her head.

"He's still committed. But he's only human. He has to take it one step at a time, one day at a time, for the rest of his life. It's times such as these when he needs a friend."

"I'm glad you are there for him, Auntie," Jenny said, giving Star a hug.

Chapter 17

Jenny went to meet Linda. Even though Linda could get up and walk a few steps, Jenny guessed she wasn't capable of driving a car to come meet her.

The constant questioning by the police had taken a toll on Linda. Jenny found her seated in her wheelchair again, in her favorite spot by the windows.

"Are you feeling alright?" Jenny asked with concern.

"I'm fine," Linda dismissed. "Just tired. I need to build up my strength."

Jenny decided against mentioning the wheelchair.

"My legs feel shaky," Linda volunteered. "My therapist has advised me to use the wheelchair for a while."

A maid served them lemonade and cookies.

"Do you have any fresh information?" Linda asked Jenny. "I could do with some good news."

"Did Asher have any other names?" she asked.

"I called him Ash sometimes," Linda said shyly. "But he preferred Asher."

"What about a middle name, maybe?"

Linda shook her head.

"What about Olga? Surely Cohen was her married name? What about before she met Asher?"

"We rarely talked about Olga."

"Who named your kids?" Jenny asked.

"Ryan's named after my grandfather. Scott was popular at the time. Dawn was my mother's name."

"What about the older kids?"

"I guess Olga named them," Linda said.

"So one or more of them could have been named after Asher's ancestors?"

"What's this sudden fascination with names?" Linda asked, leaning forward in her chair. "Are you hiding something from me?"

Jenny clasped her hands together and pursed her lips.

"I found something strange."

"Go on…"

"Asher Cohen may have been an assumed name."

"What?" Linda burst out. "How is that possible? I have known Asher ever since he came to Pelican

Cove."

"He may have taken the name before he came here," Jenny said softly.

"Why would he do that?"

"I don't know. I'm hoping to find something that may lead us to his real identity."

"I know you have built up a reputation," Linda said solicitously. "But you are wrong this time."

"Do you mind if I talk to Walter about this?"

"The older kids aren't too crazy about you," Linda confessed. "Who knows what they will say about this."

"Let me worry about that," Jenny said.

Walt was lounging in a cabana by the pool, wearing his usual uniform of khaki shorts and floral shirt. Emma and Heidi were in the pool.

"Do you have a minute?" Jenny asked Walter.

"I was about to take a nap," Walt grumbled.

"This won't take long," Jenny promised. "Do you remember anything about your life in Switzerland, or your journey here to the United States?"

Walt rolled his eyes.

"I was two, so the answer is no."

"There must have been stories about the voyage? Your mother must have talked about their life over in Switzerland?"

"If she did, I don't remember. But my mother wasn't much of a talker."

"Weren't you curious? Did you ask Asher about where you came from?"

"No. My father never talked about his family. Neither did my mother."

"You never wondered why?"

"I may have done as a child. But as I got older, I understood it was taboo."

"Taboo in what way?"

"I think it was painful for them. My father made it clear he didn't want to dwell in the past. He was too busy working anyway. My mother was busy raising kids, and giving birth to them. Five kids in ten years is a lot."

"So your father never mentioned any other names? Grandparents, uncles, aunts, friends?"

"Nope," Walter said. He closed his eyes and pulled a

hat over his face. "Bye bye."

Jenny stood up reluctantly. Emma and Heidi waved at her from the pool. Walt's wife came out with a platter of canapés. The women in the pool started climbing out when they saw the tray of food.

Jenny went to the seafood market on her way home. Chris Williams was busy doing something on his phone.

"Jenny!" he cried when he saw her. "Look what I'm doing."

Chris had registered on a few online dating sites. He had posted a flattering photo. Jenny was sure he would be getting dozens of Likes and girls would be lining up to meet him.

"I thought you were going to take the high road," she teased.

"I thought about it," he said. "But I need to beat Heather at her own game."

"What does that mean?"

"I can be popular too, you know," he said sullenly. "These portals list the most popular profiles on the top. And these profiles are suggested to other people. Just imagine Heather's face when my photo pops up on her screen. Huh?"

"You kids!" Jenny exclaimed, shaking her head. "You need to get away from everything and spend some time with each other, really think about what you want from your relationship."

"I'm all for it," Chris argued. "You know it's Heather who's not sure."

"Why don't you take her out on a romantic date?" Jenny asked. "Just the two of you?"

"Heather did mention a moonlight canoe ride," Chris reasoned. "But that was a few months ago."

"Did you forget?" Jenny asked.

"I've been busy here at the store," Chris mumbled. "Do you think she's mad at me because of that?"

Jenny shrugged and picked up a shopping basket.

"There's only one way to find out. Now tell me, do you have any fresh shrimp? Nicky's coming home for the weekend and I am cooking his favorite dinner."

Adam Hopkins came in for breakfast the next morning.

"Good Morning," Jenny greeted him. "Muffin and coffee?"

"Actually, Jenny, I'm starving. How about one of your

crab omelets?"

Jenny placed a steaming platter in front of him a few moments later. Adam bit into a piece of crispy bacon and thanked Jenny.

"How was your trip into town?" he asked. "Any luck?"

"Not really," she said evasively.

"Are you hiding something from me?" Adam asked with a hint of humor in his eyes.

"I can ask you the same thing," Jenny shot back.

"You know I can't talk about an ongoing investigation," Adam said pompously. It was his usual line. "But you don't have any such restrictions. You can discuss anything with me."

Adam speared a big piece of omelet and chewed it with gusto.

"This is so delicious, Jenny. You should start charging more for your food."

"You're trying to sidetrack me," Jenny accused. "Do you still think Linda is guilty?"

Adam put his fork down and sighed.

"I don't think so. But I have to question her based on

the evidence. I may pursue a different direction though."

"Is it another family member?" Jenny asked.

"You can say that," Adam murmured.

"Who is it?" Jenny pressed. "Is it Hans? Have you checked his alibi?"

"Hans went to buy booze for the party like he said. But he took a bit longer than expected to do that."

"What does that mean?"

"It means we haven't completely cleared him, Jenny."

"But you're not talking about Hans…"

"You will find out soon enough," Adam said cryptically.

The Magnolias breezed in at their usual time. Heather's mouth was twisted in a frown.

"What are you sulking about?" Jenny asked her.

"Chris is trying to be one up on me," she complained. "His profile popped up on my screen this morning!"

"He's doing the same thing you are," Jenny smiled.

"I warned you about this," Molly added.

"He's using an old photo," Heather cried. "No wonder he's getting so many Likes."

"In case you haven't noticed," Jenny whispered in her ear, "Chris is a handsome guy."

"He's going to be flooded with dates, old photo or not!" Molly nodded.

Jason came in for lunch, looking preoccupied.

"Got a minute?" he asked Jenny.

"Why don't you take a break and eat something?" Petunia suggested. "I can watch the counter for some time."

Jason asked for the special, a crab salad sandwich with a cup of chilled gazpacho. Jenny got the same for herself. She took the food out to the deck. It was a hot day but the cool breeze rolling off the ocean provided some respite.

"How I wish I could take a dip and cool off," Jason wailed.

"It's Friday!" Jenny reminded him. "You can do that tomorrow."

Jason ate the cold gazpacho with a spoon and took a big bite of his sandwich.

"I'm guessing the news hasn't reached you yet."

"What news?"

"The police brought Todd Buckler in for questioning today."

"Who's Todd Buckler?"

"Keep up, Jenny," Jason said. "He's Dawn's husband."

"The farmer guy?"

"That's right."

"Are you representing him too?"

Jason shook his head.

"I can't. Not while I'm Linda's lawyer. There could be a conflict of interest."

"Adam was here this morning," Jenny told Jason. "I think he hinted about this."

"Todd doesn't have an alibi."

"Wasn't he in the crowd with his little girl?"

"He stepped away for some time. Supposedly, he was getting ice cream for her."

"And he wasn't?"

Jason shrugged.

"That may not be the only thing against him."

Jenny sipped her soup and looked at Jason. Todd hadn't made much of an impression on her. He seemed quite dull compared to the rest of the Cohen family.

"What's he done?"

"His farm is in trouble," Jason told Jenny. "He's taken a second mortgage on it for some business expenses. He missed the last two payments."

"What happens if he loses the farm?"

"I don't think they will starve," Jason mused. "Asher's will takes care of Dawn. But none of his money can go to the farm."

"I'm guessing Todd didn't know that?"

"No. He's attached to that farm. Something about a deathbed promise to his father."

"You think he asked Asher for help?"

"I know he did," Jason said. "Linda told me about it. It seems Dawn is not happy on the farm. Todd runs it like a homestead. Dawn has to work hard from dawn to dusk, churning butter, collecting eggs and doing all kinds of grunt work."

"Didn't she know what she was signing up for when she married him?"

"I guess not. Or she didn't realize how hard it would actually be."

"What did Asher want?"

"Asher wanted Todd to give up the farm. He offered him a job at the firm. They could live with him and Linda or get a house in town."

"Was Dawn his favorite?"

"She's a bit of a Daddy's girl," Jason agreed. "She's the youngest of the lot. The older kids didn't really care for Linda. So they moved out as soon as they could. Ryan and Scott have their careers."

"I suppose Todd didn't want to come to Pelican Cove?"

"He doesn't want to leave his farm. It's been in his family for generations."

"So he wanted money."

Jason bit into a cupcake. It was chocolate with chocolate frosting.

"Asher had a solution. He would buy the farm and rent it out to Todd's cousin. The cousin would work the farm and Todd and Dawn would move to Pelican Cove."

"The farm stayed in the family that way."

"Right," Jason nodded. "At least Asher thought so."

"But Todd didn't agree."

"He is proud of being a farmer. He wants to grow crops all his life. He has a dairy herd too. He wants to make artisan cheese. He has big plans for the farm."

"None of them will matter if he has to foreclose," Jenny pointed out.

Jason banged a fist on the table.

"Exactly!"

"That's his motive," Jenny said, wide eyed.

"And he has no alibi," Jason finished.

"You really think he did this?" Jenny asked. "He seems kind of dumb."

"Appearances are deceptive," Jason pointed out. "Things don't look good for Todd."

"Or Dawn," Jenny added.

"I've known Dawn all my life," Jason said. "I don't think she's mixed up in this. Can't say the same for Todd though."

Chapter 18

Jenny and Heather drove to the city again.

"We should learn something new today," Heather said hopefully.

They were going to see a family called Gold. They were the people who had turned in the box of material with the photos.

Jenny was quiet. She didn't want to jinx it.

A young woman roughly Heather's age greeted them with a baby on her hip.

"Welcome to our home," she said cordially. "Please make yourselves comfortable."

A lanky young man with an aquiline nose joined them five minutes later.

"David Gold," he said, shaking hands with Jenny. "You already met my wife."

Jenny decided the man was in his mid thirties. He was too young to have submitted the material in 1965.

"One of our friends just passed," Jenny told him. "We are trying to find out more about his life in Germany."

She gave a brief account of Asher Cohen and his family without mentioning his name.

"A hundred years?" David Gold exclaimed. "He must have been my grandpa's age."

"Did you know your grandfather?" Jenny asked.

"He died when I was twelve," David said soberly, "just a few weeks before my bar mitzvah."

"I'm sorry," Jenny mumbled. "What about your parents?"

"My parents live in Florida," David told them.

"Do you know who donated the box to the museum?"

"That was my great aunt," David laughed. "My grandpa's sister. She used to live with us."

David answered before Jenny could ask the next question.

"She's gone too. She died a couple of years after Gramps."

"I guess you never saw the stuff your family donated?" Jenny said glumly.

"No," David shook his head. "But we have a lot more."

Jenny's eyebrows shot up.

"What do you mean?"

"My Dad found two boxes full of stuff when he cleaned the attic before moving to Florida. And I came across another box in the garage last year."

"Do you have this stuff with you?" Jenny asked eagerly. "Can I look at it?"

"Isn't that why you're here?" David's eyes twinkled as he smiled at Jenny.

David's wife came out with coffee and cookies.

"You're doing us a big favor," Jenny gushed.

"No worries," David assured her. "We do it all the time."

Jenny had no idea what he meant by that but she stayed silent.

David came out with the boxes and set them down on a table.

"I promised my wife I would mow the lawn today," he told Jenny. "Feel free to take your time."

Jenny found a stack of journals in one box, written in German.

"We can't read these anyway," she told Heather. "But I guess these belonged to the aunt. See the name here?"

The second box was full of photos. Most of the photos were faded. Some had water stains on them and others had dog's ears. But the men and women in them stood out.

"This is like stepping back in time," Heather said, looking gobsmacked. "Look at what they are wearing, Jenny."

"These are different from the ones I saw," Jenny said right away. "The people in these photos look happy."

David's wife heard her.

"These photos span several years," she explained. "Many of them were taken in the 1920s and 1930s. Before the war!"

"Who are all these people?" Jenny asked.

"David's family were well off," his wife told them. "They were one of the richest families in Munich. Their parties and soirees were legendary. All sorts of people were invited to these events."

Heather grabbed Jenny's arms and pointed out tiny details from the photos. Women dressed in jewels and shimmering gowns and men wearing dinner jackets and uniforms were surrounded by lavish buffet tables and waiters serving champagne. The people in the photos were laughing without a single care in the world.

Jenny put her finger on a short, stocky man with a broken nose.

"This is him," she whispered to Heather.

Jenny turned the photo around and found some names written on the back. 'Asher Cohen' was one of them. Jenny set the photo aside and rifled through the rest of the pictures. The man appeared in several photos. She set them all aside. Some of them labeled him as Asher Cohen. Some didn't have any legend at the back.

"Do you believe me now?" she asked Heather.

Heather was feeling out of her depth. She just shrugged and said nothing.

"Do you know who this is?" Jenny asked David's wife.

David Gold came in just then. He had worked up a sweat. He excused himself for a minute and came back, wiping himself off with a towel.

He looked at the photo and flipped it over.

"Oh, Asher! He was one of my grandpa's close friends."

"Do you know where he is now?" Jenny asked eagerly.

"We don't know," David said. "Grandpa didn't wait around till the end. He had the means to buy passage for his entire family and he used them. His friends weren't so lucky. Some of them were too optimistic. Many didn't believe things would deteriorate that much."

"How many people have seen these photos?" Jenny asked.

"Dozens," David told them. "Grandpa and Dad both belonged to an association of Holocaust survivors. They had quarterly meetings. People talked about their experiences, swapped stories. These boxes were brought out every time."

"What about this box you found recently?" Jenny inquired.

"I have continued the tradition," David told her proudly. "We still have meetings here, even after Dad moved to Florida. I'm the third generation Gold living in this house, you see. I bought it from my Dad."

"Have you ever been to Pelican Cove?" Jenny asked.

"Never heard of it," David said glibly.

"Can I take a couple of pictures of these photos?" Jenny asked. "I want to show them to someone."

"Sure," David shrugged. "People used to get photocopies earlier. But there's no need for that now, of course."

Jenny thanked David Gold for his time. Heather groaned when they got into the car.

"My head's reeling," she complained. "What was all that about? Why didn't you tell him your friend's name was also Asher Cohen?"

"I don't trust that man," Jenny spit out. "Don't you see? His family had ties with the real Asher Cohen."

"So what?"

"We don't know what happened to the real Asher Cohen," Jenny thought out loud. "I guess no one did for a long time."

"What are you thinking?" Heather asked.

"What if David Gold or his father came across our Asher? They would know he was an impostor."

"So what?" Heather argued. "Is that enough of a reason to kill him?"

"We need to find out if David Gold ever came to Pelican Cove."

"He said he didn't, Jenny."

"He could be lying!" Jenny wailed. "Pay attention, Heather."

"How are you going to find that out?" Heather asked. "And before you ask, no, I don't think he ever stayed at the Bayview Inn."

"What about other hotels in the area?" Jenny shot back. "I might need your help with this, Heather."

Being an inn owner, Heather was part of a local group of inn keepers. They helped each other out in need.

"Okay," Heather sighed. "I will send an email to the group. If David ever visited the area, we'll find out soon enough."

"That's all I want," Jenny smiled.

"Why did you click those photos?"

"For Linda," Jenny explained. "I want to show them to her, just in case."

Jenny wondered if Linda knew the man in the photo by another name. But that didn't make any sense to her either.

"So was this trip useful?" Heather asked. "Or are we back where we started?"

"We have a suspect outside the family," Jenny said.

"What's the motive?"

"I don't know," Jenny admitted. "Some old vendetta? Maybe Asher Cohen wasn't a friend of the Gold family. We only have David's word for it."

"How does that matter?" Heather argued. "Our Asher isn't the real Asher anyway."

"Oh, right!" Jenny said, rolling her eyes. "That's it. Let's talk about something else."

Jenny had a quiet dinner with her aunt that evening. Jimmy didn't join them that night.

"Where's Jimmy?" Jenny asked.

Her aunt's expression hardened but she didn't say anything.

"Don't be too tough on him," Jenny told her. "He needs you."

"He needs the bottle more," Star said curtly. "He's made his choice clear."

"That's harsh," Jenny said.

"I've been alone all these years," Star said. "I'm used to it. Why complicate things?"

"Do you like Jimmy?" Jenny asked.

"I like him," Star nodded. "The question is, should I let him uproot my life?"

"That depends on how much you like him," Jenny said sagely. "You told me yourself – he has to take it one day at a time. I think that applies to you too if you want to support him. Every day is going to bring fresh challenges for the both of you."

"Do you think I'm too old?" Star asked miserably.

Jenny read between the lines.

"You're never too old for love," she smiled. "You are a strong woman, Star. I know you can do this."

A tear rolled down Star's cheek. Jenny got up and hugged her aunt.

"You can do this," she whispered as she kissed the top of her head.

Jenny stepped out for her walk, hoping to run into Adam.

Jenny breathed in the familiar scent of roses from Seaview's garden. She decided she would invite Star to live with her at Seaview. They could always rent out Star's cottage.

Adam was throwing a ball for Tank, his yellow Labrador. Tank abandoned the ball as soon as he saw

Jenny. He put his paws on her shoulders and licked her nose.

"Get off me, you brute," Jenny laughed, kissing Tank on the head.

"How was your trip to the city?" Adam asked Jenny. "Any luck?"

"Too soon to say," Jenny said, trying to sound noncommittal. "What about Todd, Asher's son-in-law?"

"He's our top suspect now," Adam said grimly. "You'll probably hear this through the grapevine so I don't mind telling you. Todd had a big argument with Asher the day before the party. This was at the Rusty Anchor. Dozens of people saw them."

"So what?" Jenny asked.

"He warned the old man to lay off or else…"

"What does the family think?"

"That old guy came to see me," Adam said. "The one who lives in Florida?"

"Walter?" Jenny asked.

"Right. The siblings are not too keen on Todd. They think Dawn married down. She's better off ditching him and coming to live with Linda."

"That's all fine," Jenny said. "But what about Dawn?"

"I'm talking to her tomorrow," Adam told her.

"You mean you're bringing her in?" Jenny asked. "Is Dawn a suspect too?"

"You know how the police work," Adam sighed. "Everyone is a suspect until I clear them."

"This whole Asher business might take a different turn," Jenny said.

"Are you still thinking this is a hate crime?" Adam burst out. "That's a fantastic theory, Jenny."

"I don't know what to think any more," Jenny admitted. "This whole thing's a big mess."

"My money's on the family," Adam said. "There's just too many of them, and they had plenty of reasons to kill the old man."

"Let's forget about them for a while," Jenny said.

She sat down in the sand and stared at the ocean. The waves came up to her toes and receded, leaving a layer of foam behind.

Adam settled down next to her. Tank squeezed in

between them and Adam pushed him away.

"Why haven't we had dinner again?" he asked her.

"That's because you haven't asked me out on a second date, Adam Hopkins."

Chapter 19

"I sent an email to the group," Heather told Jenny.

The Magnolias were having coffee and tasting a batch of warm donuts Jenny had just fried up. It was a new recipe she was working on.

"Add sprinkles on top," Molly advised. "Donuts always look good with sprinkles."

"They don't really add any taste," Betty Sue argued. "What's wrong with a plain glazed donut?"

Jenny ignored the usual chatter and pulled Heather aside.

"When do you think you will hear back from them?"

"Hard to say," Heather said with a shrug.

"I better go see Linda," Jenny said resolutely. "You fancy a swim?"

Jason ended up accompanying Jenny to the Cohen estate that afternoon.

"What's your excuse to come with me?" Jenny asked.

"I need Linda's signatures on some papers," he said. "And I don't need an excuse. She's my aunt."

Linda was happy to see them. She wore a cheery smile that day and Jenny was glad to see her looking so buoyant.

"Anything new?" she asked Jenny. "The police are talking to Dawn today. As if my Dawn would do anything to harm her father."

"I want to show you some pictures," Jenny told her.

She pulled up the photos on her phone and handed them over to Linda.

"Who are all these people?" Linda asked, bewildered.

"They might have been Asher's friends," Jenny said. "From way back when he was in Germany."

"He never talked about that time," Linda said. "I already told you that."

"I know," Jenny soothed. "But some of these people might have come to America, just like Asher did. Why don't you take a look?"

Linda peered at the photos, shaking her head.

"Boy, these folks look weird."

"Anyone you know?" Jenny prompted.

She held herself from actually pointing out the real

Asher. She didn't want to bias Linda.

"Never laid eyes on any of these."

"Are you sure?"

"Yes, Jenny, I'm sure."

Jenny tried to hide her disappointment.

"What's special about these pictures?" Linda asked. "And where did you get them?"

"It's a long story," Jenny mumbled.

Jason led her to the pool. Walter, Emma and Heidi sat under a canvas awning, sipping sundowners. Todd Buckler was in the water with his little girl. He glared at Jenny and turned his back on her.

"What's the story behind those photos?" Jason asked her as he slipped on his goggles.

"Let's talk on the way back," Jenny promised.

Jason whistled when he heard Jenny's story.

"Do you think it's all too farfetched?" Jenny challenged him.

"It's amazing what you come up with, Jenny," he said. "Are you saying Linda's name isn't Cohen?"

"I don't know about that," Jenny admitted. "Linda's husband may have entered the country with this name. So it's his official name alright. You're the lawyer, Jason."

"I know," Jason groaned. "But this is all so convoluted."

"I'm going to try and get to the bottom of this," Jenny promised. "Heather might have some update."

"Let's go to the Bayview Inn then."

Jason and Jenny hurried inside the inn. Heather shook her head as soon as she saw Jenny.

"Most of the group members have replied," she told her. "None of them had David Gold as a guest."

"What if he registered under a false name?" Jenny demanded.

Heather grimaced. "Don't make this more complicated."

"I'm just thinking of the possibilities," Jenny shot back. "I think David Gold is involved."

"Want me to do a background search?" Jason offered. "I can get someone to do it for me."

"Not yet," Jenny stalled. "I'm going to try an ordinary

Internet search first."

"Why don't we grab some dinner and go to your place?" Jason suggested.

The trio headed to Mama Rosa's, the best and only pizza place in town. Jason ordered two large pies. Jenny forced him to add some salads to the order.

"What about dessert?"

"I have some leftover chocolate cake at home," Jenny told him.

Jimmy Parsons was back on the porch of Star's cottage. Jenny was relieved to see them both smiling. Her aunt had apparently reconciled with Jimmy.

Jimmy mouthed a silent thank you when she handed him a plate piled with salad and pizza. She knew he was thanking her for more than the food.

"Why don't we finish eating first?" Jason suggested between bites of pizza.

Jenny finally fired up her laptop and ran a search for David Gold.

"It's a common name," Jenny wailed as she stared at the thousands of results the computer threw back at her. "There seems to be a David Gold in every profession."

"Calm down," Jason advised. "You know where this guy lives, right? Why don't you narrow it down by location?"

"Forget all this," Heather said. "Just check on social media."

Jenny surrendered and loaded up a popular social media portal. After a few attempts, she hit pay dirt.

"This is him alright," she said, looking at a young man with a familiar aquiline nose.

He was smiling into the camera, holding a baby in his arms.

"We are in luck," Heather squealed. "He has posted plenty of photos."

Jenny clicked through photos of David and his family. There were photos of him and his wife on vacation in various exotic places. Then there were photos with the baby. Jenny could watch the child growing up in the photos.

"Looks like they haven't taken too many vacations since the baby was born," Jason observed.

"A baby ties you down," Jenny said knowingly.

"They just drove to nearby places," Heather said, reading the comments on the photos. "Look, here they are in Ocean City."

"Ocean City!" Jenny exclaimed. "That's close enough."

"That was a month ago," Heather pointed out.

"It proves nothing, Jenny," Jason winced.

"It shows he is familiar with the area," Jenny said.

"You are grasping at straws," Jason warned. "What are you looking for anyway?"

"I want to see if David Gold ever came to Pelican Cove. He told us he didn't."

Heather was clicking wildly on David Gold's profile, reading the names of his family members and friends. Jenny sat back and rubbed her temples, irked at reaching another dead end.

"Stop!" she cried suddenly.

She pointed at the photo of an older man.

"I know that man."

"You do?" Heather quizzed. "David has listed him as a friend."

Jenny seemed uncertain.

"I mean, I have seen him somewhere."

Jason peered at the photo Jenny was pointing at.

"Looks pretty ordinary to me, Jenny. Are you sure you saw the same man? Where did you see him?"

"I saw him recently," Jenny maintained. "It must have been at the café."

"He could have been a tourist," Jason offered.

"I've never seen him," Heather said firmly.

"Let's ask Star," Jenny pleaded. "She gets around a lot."

Star and Jimmy were summoned and shown the photo.

"What's he doing here?" Jimmy exclaimed. "That's the guy who lives in one of my cottages," he told Star. "The one who's writing that book about birds."

"Ira Brown!" Jenny gasped. "How could I forget him."

"That's right," Jimmy nodded. "He was really impressed by the lunch you gave him at the Boardwalk Café."

"You've actually met this guy?" Jason asked.

"And I'm going to meet him again tomorrow."

"I need to get home, Jenny," Heather said, stifling a yawn. "I have to cut up the fruit for tomorrow's breakfast before I turn in."

The group broke up after that.

Jenny tossed and turned all night, eager to talk to Ira Brown the next day. Jimmy had agreed to get her an appointment with the man.

Jenny was just sitting down to eat a bite herself when Jimmy called. He had promised Ira another free lunch at the café. Ira had readily accepted.

"When are you meeting that man?" Heather asked as soon as she came in for coffee with her grandma Betty Sue.

"Soon," Jenny said. "Are you free later today? I might go talk to David Gold again."

Ira Brown came in for lunch. He chose a window table and sat down, rubbing his hands in anticipation. He licked his lips and looked at Jenny greedily.

"What are you serving today?"

"Fish tacos," Jenny told him. "We got some white fish this morning."

"I can't wait," he said greedily.

Jenny set a platter down before him and sat down.

"Where do you live?" she asked. "I think you mentioned Maryland?"

Ira took a big bite of his taco and nodded his head.

"How do you know David Gold?"

"David who?" Ira asked, wiping his mouth with a paper napkin.

He seemed a bit miffed at the interruption.

"David Gold," Jenny repeated. "I met him last week when I was in the city. I noticed he has marked you as a friend."

"Don't remember the name," Ira said.

He took another big bite of his taco and chewed it slowly. Jenny let him eat.

"People know me because of my profile," he said finally. "I don't always know them."

"It's a two way connection," Jenny explained. "You don't appear as a friend unless you have accepted someone's invite."

Ira Brown's face cleared.

"Oh! I get dozens of friend requests every week. I accept all of them. Don't want to appear standoffish, you know. I have a certain image."

"So you're saying there are plenty of people out there who have listed you as a friend. But you don't know them."

"Exactly!"

"Isn't that risky?" Jenny asked. "I took you for a private person."

Ira Brown chomped on the last piece of his taco.

"You got that right," he said. "I value my privacy a lot. Why do you think I am spending my summer on this remote island?"

"I thought you were here for the birds?"

"That too," Ira Brown said quickly.

Jenny pulled up David Gold's profile on her phone. She thrust it in Ira Brown's face.

"You really don't know this guy?"

Ira Brown glanced at the photo and shook his head.

"I'm sorry. Looks like this guy's important to you."

"Not really," Jenny said with a smile. "Thanks for coming here to talk to me."

Ira smiled solicitously.

"I came here for this delicious lunch. It was worth every bite."

"How about some dessert?" Jenny asked. "I have lemon cake with berry compote."

Ira Brown lingered for a while, enjoying his dessert over two cups of coffee. Jenny watched him from behind the counter as she served other customers. He looked so calm it was hard to believe he was hiding anything.

Jenny picked up Heather and Molly and drove to the city. David Gold opened the door, holding his son in his arms.

"This is a surprise!" he said. "We were just going out." He turned around and called out to his wife. "Look who's here, honey."

"I'm sorry we didn't call before coming," Jenny apologized.

She was hoping David would invite them in. David didn't disappoint.

"Come on in," he said. "We were just going on a grocery run. It can wait."

His wife came out with a tray of lemonade. She took

the baby from David and went in.

"I was hoping to ask you a few questions," Jenny began. "We found your social profile…"

"Were you trying to look me up?" David said with a laugh. "I don't mind. I do it too."

Molly was staring at David with her mouth open. She was clearly besotted with the handsome young man.

"You went to Ocean City, didn't you?" Heather blurted out.

"That was over a month ago," David nodded. "We didn't want to go too far from home with the baby."

"So you're familiar with the Eastern Shore?" Jenny asked.

"We were planning to drive down the peninsula," David nodded. "But that never happened. My son had an ear infection the first day out. We had to come back immediately."

"You have an admirable number of friends," Jenny began. "I might know one of them."

Chapter 20

David Gold didn't hesitate for a second after he saw Ira Brown's photo.

"Professor Brown? He comes here all the time."

"He said he didn't know you," Jenny informed him.

"He's writing a book about the Holocaust," David told them. "You remember that group I told you about? He comes to our meetings."

"Would he have access to those boxes you showed us?"

"He sure does," David said. "He's even planning to use some of those photos in his book."

"Why would he lie to me?" Jenny mused. "Did you have some kind of falling out?"

David looked bewildered.

"Ira's a bit whimsical. But surely he couldn't have forgotten who I am? He's coming here this weekend for our quarterly meeting. I just got his RSVP."

"He must have been joking," Jenny soothed.

She wanted to go confront Ira Brown as soon as

possible.

Heather and Molly both protested when she passed into the exit lane for the highway.

"I have a date!" Heather exclaimed.

"Now?" Jenny burst out. "When were you going to mention that?"

"Duster texted me while you were talking to David," she said. "He's here for an errand. I'm meeting him for coffee."

"What are we supposed to do while you meet him?" Jenny asked.

"I don't know…go shopping or something."

"I could use some coffee," Molly said with a gleam in her eye.

"You are not coming to the same coffee shop," Heather cried. "I don't need chaperones."

"Who said we are with you?" Molly teased. "We'll get our own table and do our thing. Maybe I will meet a gorgeous hunk."

"How can you think of guys at a time like this?" Jenny moaned. "I feel I'm close to solving this."

"Don't get your hopes up," Heather scoffed. "So what if that old man lied to you? He doesn't owe you anything."

"People lie for a reason," Jenny said.

"Yes," Heather nodded. "And most likely it's something silly."

"We'll see," Jenny sighed.

Heather texted Duster to meet her a block away from the coffee shop. Molly and Jenny were waiting for their order.

"I might be taking a page out of Heather's book," Molly said shyly.

"Plain English, please," Jenny said, rubbing the charm around her neck.

"I downloaded that dating app Heather uses," Molly admitted. "I may be going out on a date myself."

"That's great, Molly," Jenny said brightly. "Have you shortlisted any profiles? Show me, now!"

Molly handed over her phone to Jenny. "This is the profile I like best."

Jenny took one look at it and burst out laughing.

"Are you kidding me, Molly?"

"What's wrong with him?" Molly asked seriously.

Jenny looked over her shoulder and leaned forward.

"This is Chris. Chris Williams. Heather's beau."

"He's not her beau any more if she's dating other people."

"You know they have an understanding…"

"He's put his profile out there. He's up for grabs. I'm going for it."

"What's got into you, Molly? Is this some kind of reverse psychology to get Heather back on track?"

Molly teared up.

"Heather doesn't know what she has. It's not my fault if she gives up the best thing that happened to her."

"You really want to do this?" Jenny asked incredulously.

Molly crumpled a bunch of tissues and stirred her coffee vigorously.

"I've always liked Chris."

"You mean you have a crush on him?" Jenny asked,

wide eyed. "Since when?"

"Since high school."

"But weren't you dating someone else at that time?"

"Have you seen Chris?" Molly flung her hands wide. "He was the captain of our football team and he got good grades."

Jenny recalled the old yearbooks from Heather and Molly's school days. Chris Williams had been one good looking kid.

"He's handsome ... I'll give you that."

"Handsome is as handsome does, Jenny," Molly said. "Chris is a good person."

"Won't this be awkward?"

"It's up to him," Molly shrugged. "He will handle Heather if necessary."

Jenny tried to size up the girl sitting before her. Molly was tall and scrawny. The Coke-bottle glasses she wore made her eyes look frog like. She barely paid any attention to her appearance. But she had a heart of gold.

"Go for it," she said softly.

"You mean it?" Molly asked eagerly. "I need your support, Jenny."

"Let it play out," Jenny advised. "But be prepared for any consequences."

"I know I barely have a chance," Molly said meekly. "But I need to give it a shot."

Heather breezed in before they could say anything more. She had a silly smile on her face.

"Duster invited me to his beach house this weekend."

"Haven't you already been there?" Jenny asked her.

"Yes, but I am going alone this time," Heather said stoutly. "And staying over."

Jenny and Molly teased her mercilessly. Molly gave Jenny a knowing look.

Heather was craving Chinese food so they decided to get take-out from a restaurant next door.

"What's going on between your aunt and Jimmy Parsons?" Heather asked Jenny in the car.

Jenny had ordered enough food for a dozen people. Jason always got them Chinese food from the city so she had texted him to come to her place for dinner. She called Star and told her not to cook anything. She assumed Jimmy would stick around for dinner too.

"They are getting along fine," Jenny said with a smile.

"Aren't they really old?" Heather crinkled her nose.

"Age has nothing to do with love," Jenny preached. "And I think there's some history there."

"There's hope for all of us then," Molly said meaningfully.

"Yeah, even you, Molls," Heather laughed.

"You don't have to be so nasty," Molly bristled.

"Give it a rest, girls," Jenny snapped.

"Are you still thinking about that man?" Heather asked.

"I can't wait to go talk to him."

Jason was sitting on Star's porch, waiting for them.

"Finally!" he said, looking relieved.

"Something wrong?" Jenny asked, sensing his mood.

"Walt had an accident."

"Who's Walt?" Molly asked.

"Asher's oldest," Jenny reminded her. "The one who lives in a retirement community in Florida." She turned to Jason. "What happened? Is he alright?"

"Walt took his wife and sisters to Williamsburg. They were on their way back home. Someone rammed into him, tried to run him off the road."

Jenny's eyebrows shot up. "Someone's out to get Asher's family," she said.

"Hold on now," Jason said. "Let's not jump to conclusions. It could have been a crazy driver. We know the roads are full of them."

"I have a gut feeling about this," Jenny insisted. "I need to call Adam."

She dialed Adam's number and spoke to him in a rush. She hung up five minutes later, red in the face.

"He doesn't believe me."

Jason's phone rang just then. His face turned grim as he listened to the voice on the other side.

"That was Linda," he said. "Someone broke the windows of the greenhouse and pulled all the plants out of the pots."

Jenny placed her hands on her hips and glared at Jason.

"What do you say now?"

Jason was already dialing Adam.

"I'm going over to Linda's," he said, getting up. "Adam's coming there too."

"I will go with you," Jenny said.

"Sorry," Jason said. "Adam forbid me from bringing you along."

"He can't do that," Jenny roared. "I can go where I want. As long as Linda wants me there, Adam has no say in the matter."

"I am requesting you to stay put," Jason said. "Please, Jenny. We don't know what's going on. Just stay here with Star and the girls. Don't make me worry about you."

"Do you promise to give me an update as soon as you learn something?" Jenny asked.

"You are the first person I will call," Jason sighed.

He looked at Molly and Heather.

"Why don't you girls stick around? Have dinner? All that food's getting cold anyway."

Star had come out while Jason was talking. Jimmy

tagged behind her.

"Don't worry about Jenny, boy," she boomed. "I can take care of her."

Jenny was lost in thought as she ladled General Tso's chicken on to her plate. It was her favorite. Her aunt and Jimmy had both opted for the sesame chicken. Molly was munching on Crab Rangoons.

Heather twirled some lo mein noodles around her fork and looked around.

"Didn't we get some shrimp?"

"I'm saving it for Jason," Jenny said. "It's his favorite."

"And what's Adam's favorite?" Heather laughed.

"Adam likes Sichuan chicken," Jenny said with a straight face.

"Did you buy out the whole restaurant, Jenny?" Star asked. "There's enough to feed an army."

"She was thinking of Adam and Jason," Heather quipped.

"So what if I was?" Jenny asked belligerently. "We are just wasting our time here."

"What's got you rattled, girl?" Star scowled.

Jenny was quiet after that. The girls loaded the dish washer while Jenny scooped up some ice cream for dessert.

"How long has Ira Brown been living in town?" she asked Jimmy as she served the dessert.

"He rented the place in April," Jimmy said, trying to remember. "He came here around Memorial Day."

"Was he here for the July 4th holiday?"

"I think he was," Jimmy said sheepishly. "I don't remember."

Jenny realized Jimmy probably hadn't been sober at that time.

Heather snapped her fingers.

"You know what? We ran a search on David Gold but we didn't run one on this professor fellow."

"You're right," Jenny said eagerly.

She switched on her laptop and ran a search on Ira Brown. The results showed he was a professor in a small college in Maryland. He taught history and his area of research was Jewish Studies. Jenny could find no mention of birds.

"He lied to us, see?" Jenny looked up in triumph.

"He's got nothing to do with birds."

"Many people come here to watch the birds, Jenny," Star reasoned. "They want to forget about their everyday lives for a while. The birds are their escape."

"But look what he teaches at the college," Jenny pointed out. "How could he not know David Gold?"

"Didn't we already establish that?" Molly quizzed. "Who do you trust more at this point David Gold or Ira Brown?"

Jenny thought of David's frank face and open attitude. There was something guileless about him.

"I trust David," she said.

"Let's check the old man's social profile," Heather spoke up.

She pulled Jenny's laptop toward herself and began pulling up different social media portals. She pulled up a bunch of photos of Pelican Cove.

"Look at these," she said, turning the screen so that the others could see clearly. "I know all these places. They are around Pelican Cove. You need a boat to get there."

"He takes a kayak out pretty much every day," Jimmy prompted. "At least, that's what he told me."

"Any photos from July 4th?" Jenny asked.

Heather showed her a few photos of the barbecue. Ira Brown was wearing a blue vest proclaiming him to be a volunteer.

"What was he doing volunteering at the parade?" Molly asked. "Tourists don't do that."

"Ask Barb Norton," Star ordered. "She was in charge of the volunteers."

Jenny made a quick call to Barb. Barb played some part in every event that happened in Pelican Cove. Jenny spoke for a few minutes and hung up.

"Ira Brown was a volunteer on the catering crew," Jenny confirmed. "Barb said they were short of volunteers and he seemed very eager."

"That puts him on the spot," Heather said.

Jenny tried to hide her excitement.

"So where was he during the awards ceremony?"

Chapter 21

Heather got busy downloading photos off the Internet.

"What are you doing now, Heather?"

"Many people posted photos of the July 4th parade online. I am getting all of them on your computer. We can look through them and try to spot your professor."

Heather was ready with the photos a few minutes later.

"Look, these are from the parade itself," Molly pointed. "There he is, standing close to Linda."

"What's he doing there?" Jenny wondered.

They spotted Ira Brown in different places through the day. He was flipping burgers on the grill, diverting traffic, eating ice cream and sitting under the big marquee. He was easily recognizable because of his blue vest. He was alone in all the photos.

"What about the awards ceremony?" Molly asked.

"I saved the best for last," Heather said grimly.

They scrolled through dozens of photos featuring the awards ceremony. They spotted many people they knew in the crowd but Ira Brown wasn't one of them.

"Where was he, huh?" Jenny asked triumphantly.

"He could have gone to the bathroom," Star said meekly. "Why don't you talk to Barb again? She will have more photos of the whole event."

Jenny spent some time talking to Barb Norton.

"She's bringing over the photos," Jenny said as she hung up. "There was an official photographer for the whole event. If Ira was at the awards ceremony, he has to be in one of those photos."

Pelican Cove had no traffic to speak of and distances were short. Barb Norton arrived fifteen minutes later. The girls rifled through the photos while Star took Barb aside and gave her a spiel about why they needed to see the photos urgently.

The girls looked up at the same time and shook their heads.

"He has no alibi!" Jenny exclaimed. "Wanna bet he's our guy?"

Barb Norton was sent home and the girls tried to watch a movie. Jenny was restlessly awaiting some word from Jason.

"What's taking them so long?" she wailed for the third time in an hour.

Finally, they heard a car drive up outside. Jenny rushed to the door. Jason came in, followed by Adam.

"How is Linda?" Jenny burst out. "And the other Cohens?"

"Everyone is fine," Jason said. "Nobody was hurt."

Adam's face was ashen and he leaned heavily on his cane.

"Why don't you sit here?" Jenny said, pointing to an arm chair with an ottoman.

She held herself back from helping Adam. He asked her for some water and pulled out a bottle of pills from his pocket. He popped a couple of pills and sighed heavily.

"You boys must be hungry," Star said, giving Jenny a meaningful glare.

Food was heated and Jenny barely contained herself while Jason and Adam wolfed the food down.

"Wait till you hear what we found," Jenny said finally. "Ira Brown has no alibi for the awards ceremony."

"Who is Ira Brown?" Adam asked with a frown.

"Ira Brown is the top suspect. He lied to me about a lot of things. You need to bring him in for questioning."

"You can't tell me what to do, Jenny," Adam growled. "Don't interfere in police business."

"But…"

"No buts."

"You'll be sorry you didn't listen to me," Jenny said, her hands on her hips. "Ira Brown is your guy."

"I'm getting out of here," Adam barked, struggling to get up.

"Calm down," Jason said sharply. "You can both have your say."

He looked at Adam.

"Let's hear what the girls found out."

Jenny gave Adam a brief version of what she had discovered in the city. She explained how Ira Brown had access to the old photos of the real Asher and how he had lied about knowing David Gold.

"And he wasn't at the awards ceremony," Heather butted in. "Isn't that when Asher was killed?"

"You mean the man we know as Asher Cohen," Adam snorted.

"Yes, yes," Jenny snapped. "Our Asher."

Adam let her ramble on for some time. Jenny finally stopped talking.

"Are you done?" Adam asked sarcastically. "Do you want to know what we found out?"

Jason cut to the chase.

"Todd Buckler confessed."

"What?" a bunch of voices chorused.

"He had a grudge against all the Cohens. Asher wouldn't give him money and Dawn's siblings almost talked her into leaving the farm."

"So what did he do?" Jenny breathed.

"He trashed the greenhouse today," Jason explained. "He told Dawn they were through. He was fleeing back home when the police caught him."

"We have a confession," Adam repeated. "Todd was always a strong suspect. He doesn't have an alibi for the time Asher was killed."

"But did he confess to killing Asher?" Jenny demanded.

"He said he hated Asher and wanted him out of the

way."

"That's not the same as a confession."

"No, but he'll fess up eventually."

"I think you need to talk to Ira."

Jason spoke up. "I agree with Jenny. I think the man is hiding something."

Adam held up his hand.

"I'm exhausted. Let's discuss this tomorrow morning."

He thanked Star for dinner and limped out without saying a word to Jenny.

"Adam is so stubborn," Jenny fumed. "Why doesn't he believe us?"

"Let him sleep on it," Jason said mildly. "He'll come around."

"We might be too late," Jenny moaned.

Heather let out a yawn and that set everyone off. The girls left and Jason sat with Jenny on the porch.

"I wish I could take you away from all this," he murmured.

"Why?" Jenny asked. "I love it here."

She sidled closer to Jason and they sat there, staring at the waves lapping against the beach.

Jenny was up at 5 AM as usual. She headed to the café and started baking her first batch of blueberry muffins. Her favorite customer, Captain Charlie, arrived at six as usual. She chatted with him as she served him his coffee and muffin.

She reeled back in shock when the next person in line stepped up to the counter.

"Mr. Brown!"

"Good Morning," Ira Brown greeted her cheerfully. "How about that muffin?"

"You are up early," Jenny said as she wrapped his muffin for him. "Going somewhere?"

"I'm driving up to the city," Ira Brown smiled. "Got a meeting at my college."

"But you are coming back?"

"In a day or two…"

"How about a hot breakfast before you hit the road?" Jenny asked. "I'm making crab omelets."

Ira seemed to waver.

"I need to be on my way."

"It won't take long," Jenny assured him. "Why don't you have a seat? Your food will be out in a few minutes."

She rushed into the kitchen and dialed the police station.

"Adam," she said urgently. "He's getting away."

The clerk told her Adam wasn't in yet. Luckily, he walked into the café just then.

Jenny almost dragged him inside.

"That's him by the window," she whispered. "Ira Brown. He's leaving town. You need to talk to him now!"

"I thought about what you said," Adam nodded. "You may have a point."

"You want to let him eat first?"

"Let him have his last supper," Adam quipped.

Adam Hopkins sat at a table near Ira Brown, enjoying his own omelet. He stood up as soon as he saw Ira push his plate aside.

Jenny watched from the counter as Adam spoke to the

man. Ira shook his head from side to side and waved his arms in the air. Finally, his head dropped as he seemed to give in. Adam took him by the arm and ushered him outside.

The phone in the kitchen rang ten minutes later.

"You want to sit in on this?" Adam asked.

Jenny almost ran the two blocks to the police station. Nora, the desk clerk, waved her through. Ira sat in a small room, tapping his fingers on the desk. Adam came out and spoke to Jenny.

"He admits being a volunteer at the July 4th event. He says he attended the awards ceremony."

"Then why isn't he in any of the photos?"

"He was backstage."

"That's a lie!"

Adam shrugged.

"I have nothing to hold him here, really. Is there anything you want to ask him?"

"Adam Hopkins!" Jenny exclaimed. "Are you actually allowing me to question a suspect? Isn't that part of police business?"

"Just this once, Jenny," Adam warned. "Don't get used to it."

Jenny entered the room and sat down next to Adam. Ira Brown was surprised to see her.

"What are you doing here?"

Jenny didn't beat around the bush.

"You lied to me about David Gold."

"David who?"

Jenny pulled out her phone and began dialing David.

Ira held up a hand.

"I know him, okay. So what?"

"Why are you here in Pelican Cove?"

"I'm here for the birds. I am writing a book on birds of the Delmarva."

"So you are a bird professor? What do they call them, ornithologist?"

Ira Brown leaned back in his chair before he answered.

"I teach a lot of things. Let's say the birds are a hobby."

"You are a professor of Jewish Studies, aren't you?" Jenny challenged.

Ira shrugged.

"Why did you volunteer for the July 4th parade?"

"I like to keep busy. The long weekend can get kind of lonely for a single person like me. It was a way to be around people."

"Oh?" Jenny said. "Have you made any friends in town?"

"I met a few people," Ira said.

"Was Asher Cohen one of them?"

"You mean that 100 year old guy? He was a bit hoity toity."

Jenny wrote something on a piece of paper and handed it to Adam. Adam read it, nodded, and stepped out.

Jenny waited until he came back.

"Are you writing a book about the Holocaust?" she resumed a few minutes later.

"Who told you that?" Ira asked. "I'm just getting started."

"What kind of research are you doing for it?"

"How is that relevant?" Ira demanded. "Why am I here, anyway?" He pointed a finger at Adam. "You can't just keep me here and ask these nonsensical questions."

"You saw the old photos that David Gold has, didn't you?" Jenny pushed on. "You saw the photo of a man called Asher Cohen."

Ira said nothing.

"You saw an opportunity to blackmail an old man. You asked him for money. When he didn't agree, you killed him in a fit of rage."

Ira laughed.

"You're crazy. Most of those photos are faded. And they are from before the war."

"And they show Jewish people living in luxury," Jenny snapped. "You couldn't take that, could you? You came here and saw another Jew living a life of luxury. You couldn't tolerate that. So you killed him."

"You have it all wrong," Ira Brown said.

"I know I'm right, Mr. Brown. You are an antisemite. That's why you killed Asher Cohen."

Ira Brown's eyes bulged in disbelief.

"Me? An antisemite? My grandfather was at Auschwitz. I grew up hearing stories of Nazi brutality. Do you understand? And I am Jewish myself. Have you forgotten that? How can I be an antisemite?"

There was a knock on the door. Someone handed a note over to Adam. Adam's face changed as he read it. He looked at Ira with a sneer.

"You went fishing with Asher Cohen. You knew him well. We have a witness who saw you talking to him after the parade."

"So why did you kill a fellow Jew?" Jenny asked.

Ira Brown banged his fist on the table. His ears had turned red.

"He wasn't a Jew," he thundered.

Then he sang like a canary.

Chapter 22

Linda Cohen sat on a couch with her youngest daughter Dawn by her side. The other Cohen clan sat on chairs and couches around the big parlor. Emma and Heidi huddled close together and Walt had an arm around his wife's shoulders. Luke Stone leaned against a table.

Jenny took a deep breath before she spoke. Jason patted her on the shoulder, giving her an encouraging look.

"Hello everyone," Jenny began. "Thanks for coming."

"Why is she calling a meeting?" Heidi grumbled. "Haven't we suffered enough?"

"Be quiet, Heidi," Walt ordered. "None of this would have come to light without her help. We owe her."

"Owe her what? A lifetime of disgrace?" Heidi muttered.

"That's enough, Heidi," Linda said. "Go on, Jenny."

"Ira Brown killed your father," Jenny told Walt. "He gave a full confession."

"And he did it because our father was a Nazi?" Emma

asked.

"It appears so," Jenny said.

"Can you tell us the whole story?" Linda requested. "Please?"

"I can tell you what I pieced together," Jenny said. "There may still be some missing elements."

A heavy silence settled around the room as Jenny began her story.

"Let's refer to your father as Asher for the sake of simplicity," Jenny started.

"Apparently, Asher was an officer in Hitler's army. He used the name of Asher Cohen to escape to Switzerland and later come to America. He spent his whole life under that name. As you all know, he had a family, a business, a normal life. He never spoke much about his past. He didn't have any obvious religious affiliations, preferring to immerse himself in his work."

"Where does Ira Brown come in?" Heidi asked.

"Ira Brown is the son of Jewish immigrants. His grandfather was a Holocaust survivor. Ira grew up listening to tales of Nazi brutality. He chose Jewish Studies as his subject and did more research on that period in history. We can say he was completely immersed in it."

"So he hated Nazis with a vengeance," Walt nodded.

"I suppose we can say that," Jenny agreed. "Some of what Ira Brown told us was true. He rented a cottage here on the island for the summer. He wanted a break from his usual life. He is an avid bird watcher. He had planned to spend the summer studying the birds of the region. He was looking forward to a quiet summer."

"How did he meet my Asher?" Linda asked.

Jenny looked at Jason and shrugged.

"We don't know that for sure. He might have run into him somewhere in town."

"That's right," Luke Stone spoke up. "Asher met him at the bait and tackle shop. They got talking about fishing."

"I guess Asher invited him to fish in our creek?" Linda asked sadly.

"Yes," Luke said. "They met a few times. Asher told him about the centennial and even invited him to the party at our house."

"It's all pretty straightforward so far," Walt said. "What went wrong?"

"Ira Brown knew this man called David Gold. David's grandfather was also a Holocaust survivor. His family escaped before the war. They had plenty of keepsakes in the form of journals and old photographs. David played an active part in some Jewish association. They brought those photos out during the meetings. People liked to see the photos and talk about the good old days, days when their ancestors were rich and famous and led lavish lives in Germany. Ira attended these meetings."

"He saw those photos?" Heidi asked, now drawn into the story.

Jenny nodded. "We can only guess."

"And you think my Asher was in one of them?" Linda asked.

"I have seen those photos," Jenny told the assembled people. "They are old and faded but you wouldn't believe the life they depict. Extravagant parties, ladies decked in jewels, men in dinner suits and uniforms – all kinds of people congregated at these functions. One of the men appeared in a few photos. The writing at the back labeled him as Asher Cohen."

"But he wasn't our father?" Walt burst out.

"No, he wasn't," Jenny said, shaking her head. "That was the first clue I got."

"Is that all?" Linda asked. "My husband could have used the name for any reason. Why did this Ira Brown murder him?"

"Call it fate or coincidence," Jenny explained, "but Ira Brown got to know our Asher pretty well. He spotted him in the old photos, wearing a uniform. The enemy's uniform, as he called it. He just saw red after that. He assumed our Asher killed or tortured the real Asher Cohen and hid out here. As far as Ira Brown is concerned, our Asher was a war criminal and deserved to be punished."

"Why didn't he turn him over to the police?" Walt asked.

"Who knows?" Jenny shrugged. "He had strong feelings on the subject. He said he wanted justice. He wanted to avenge the life of every poor Jew who ever suffered under the hands of the Nazis."

Linda dabbed her eyes with a lace handkerchief.

"Did he plan it all?"

"He tried to. He got more desperate as the centennial drew close. He volunteered for the July 4th event, hoping he wouldn't be noticed if he was dressed like the locals. He was right in a way."

Luke Stone stood behind Linda and placed his hands on her shoulders.

"Are you sure you want to hear about this?"

"Yes," Linda said bravely. "I want to know about my Asher's last moments."

Jenny cleared her throat.

"It's not pretty," she warned. "Ira said he wanted the man to suffer just like all those folks who were killed back in Germany. He sought Asher out during the awards ceremony and led him to his car. He had already rigged the car up so it became a gas chamber. He held Asher at gunpoint, forcing him to stay in the car and inhale all that smoke."

Jenny stopped talking after that. Linda let out a sob.

"I wasn't too crazy about the old man," Walt said soberly. "But surely nobody deserves that?"

"What if he did?" Heidi exclaimed. "What if he was responsible for killing innocent people all those years ago?"

"We'll never know about that," Emma whispered.

"I don't know who my husband was before he came to this country," Linda said strongly. "But I know who he was here. He loved his family. He built up a business that supported hundreds of other families in the region. He led an honorable life. You will talk about him with respect."

"Isn't that too much to ask?" Heidi protested.

"Actually, it isn't," Jason spoke up. "I have something for you."

He held up an envelope and waved it in front of the assembled group.

"You know I was Asher's lawyer. He left a letter for all of you. I was supposed to reveal its existence only under certain conditions. I think those conditions have been met."

"Have you read it?" Jenny asked him, wide eyed.

"I have," Jason nodded. "I'm sorry Jenny, it's addressed to the family."

"Let her read it," Linda said, looking around the room.

"Sure," Walt said.

Heidi grunted her assent.

"Why don't you tell us what it says, Jason?" Linda suggested.

"Is he innocent or isn't he?" Heidi interrupted.

"Hold on, Heidi," Walt said.

He looked at Jason and gave a nod. "Just tell us what's in it."

"I won't read it word for word," Jason started. "You

can all do that later. I'm going to tell you the story at a high level. Our Asher was from Munich. He joined the army at a young age and later became a Major. The social environment before the war was different. Some Jews were in prominent positions. Wealthy Jewish families held parties where all kinds of people mingled with each other. Our guy was friendly with many of these people."

"Does he say anything about his family?" Walt asked.

Jason nodded.

"He had a younger sister and mother. His father died when he was ten."

"Go on," Linda urged.

"Well, the atrocities started. Jewish businesses closed down. Some of them left the cities. Others escaped the country. Things got worse and it got more and more difficult to get away."

"Our father continued to work for the army?" Walt asked.

"I don't know how he managed it. But he hid a few people in his house. He writes about it in his letter. Six Jews lived in his basement for over a year. One of them was Asher Cohen, a good friend of your father. All this time, your father was trying to arrange papers for their escape."

Heidi gasped but said nothing.

"Those were hard times. They managed to get away. I won't go into details of their journey. The letter skims over that. They encountered the German forces somewhere along the way. The Germans shot at them. Your father's mother and sister were killed in the skirmish along with some of their group. Your father escaped with a young woman called Olga. They entered Switzerland as a couple. Your father had Asher Cohen's papers with him. He just went with that name."

"So our mother was really Jewish?" Walt asked.

"She was your father's neighbor. Her family were one of the first to be rounded up in the area. Your grandmother took her in and hid her."

"Why didn't he resume his real identity when he came to America?" Heidi asked.

"He wanted to honor his old friend Asher. And he didn't want to forget what happened."

The family threw more questions at Jason and he answered all of them. Linda read the letter while they discussed its shocking contents. She handed it over to Walt. The mood in the room grew somber as everyone read the letter one by one.

"Poor Dad," Emma sighed. "He was as strong as an

ox. He would easily have lived many more years."

"Curse the day Ira Brown ever came to Pelican Cove," Luke Stone said.

Jenny sat back, barely listening to the siblings. The whole thing felt too bizarre for words. She had come to one conclusion. Life was fickle and you never knew what lay around the next corner. All you could do was grab it by the horns and live each moment like it was your last.

Epilogue

Jenny sat on the deck of the Boardwalk Café, staring at the ocean. Adam Hopkins sat in a chair beside her, holding her hand. Jason Stone stood behind her with his hands on her shoulders.

The Magnolias had decided to have a potluck at the café that weekend. Dozens of dishes were crammed on two tables, and a delicious aroma rose up in the air.

Star sat on the steps leading to the beach. Jimmy Parsons sat huddled next to her, one arm around her shoulders. The other hand fed her a roasted chicken leg. Both of them looked happy.

"Where did you say Heather was?" Betty Sue Morse called out, wiping barbecue sauce off her fingers. "I don't know why she had to run errands today."

Heather had gone on a date with Duster. Her grandmother was still in the dark about her recent exploits.

Molly and Chris sat at another table, trying to make small talk. Jenny had high hopes for them.

"What's next for you, Jenny?" Adam asked.

"Luke and his men have started repairs on Seaview," she told him. "I can't wait to move in."

"You're not afraid?" Adam asked. "It's supposed to be haunted."

"Yeah, right!" Jenny laughed.

Jason got up to get them some pie.

"How about dinner tomorrow night?" Adam asked her.

Jenny's face fell.

"Rain check?"

"Let me guess, you're going out with Jason."

"He asked first."

THE END

Thank you for reading this book. If you enjoyed this book, please consider leaving a brief review. Even a few words or a line or two will do.

As an indie author, I rely on reviews to spread the word about my book. Your assistance will be very helpful and greatly appreciated.

I would also really appreciate it if you tell your friends and family about the book. Word of mouth is an author's best friend, and it will be of immense help to me.

Many Thanks!

Author Leena Clover

http://leenaclover.com

Leenaclover@gmail.com

http://twitter.com/leenaclover

https://www.facebook.com/leenaclovercozymysterybooks

Other books by Leena Clover

Pelican Cove Cozy Mystery Series –

Strawberries and Strangers

Berries and Birthdays

Sprinkles and Skeletons

Waffles and Weekends

Muffins and Mobsters

Parfaits and Paramours

Meera Patel Cozy Mystery Series -

Gone with the Wings

A Pocket Full of Pie

For a Few Dumplings More

Back to the Fajitas

Christmas with the Franks

Acknowledgements

A big thank you to all my beta readers and advanced readers for their invaluable feedback and support. This one was a bit harder to write and I couldn't have done it without my friend Bob's help.

As always, my heartfelt thanks and gratitude to my ever loving family.

Join my Newsletter

Get access to exclusive bonus content, sneak peeks, giveaways and much more. Also get a chance to join my exclusive ARC group, the people who get first dibs on all my new books.

Sign up at the following link and join the fun.

Click here → http://www.subscribepage.com/leenaclovernl

I love to hear from my readers, so please feel free to connect with me at any of the following places.

Website – http://leenaclover.com

Twitter – https://twitter.com/leenaclover

Facebook – http://facebook.com/leenaclovercozymysterybooks

Email – leenaclover@gmail.com

Printed in Great Britain
by Amazon